Chasing the Prize

Michele Shriver

SMC Publishing

Chasing the Prize: A Men of the Ice Novella
By Michele Shriver
Copyright 2016 Michele Shriver
Published by SMC Publishing
All Rights Reserved

ISBN-13:
978-1534664838

ISBN-10:
1534664831

"You do not play hockey for good seasons. You play to win the Stanley Cup. It has to be the objective."- Guy Lafleur

CHAPTER ONE

Ryder Carrigan sat on a stage in the San Antonio Events center and tried to mentally prepare himself for the torture that would soon follow. He was a student of history, and could offer a list of the some of the worst forms of torture ever known to man. Impalement, drawing and quartering, heretics fork, white torture, waterboarding. All were awful, yet none compared to what Ryder was about to endure on this mid-September Friday evening.

The San Antonio Generals Charity Foundation Bachelor Auction.

Or, as Ryder referred to it, fresh meat for slaughter.

As a professional hockey player, there were a number of things expected of Ryder. For example, as one of the Generals' Alternate Captains, he was expected to make himself available to the media following games, and to answer their questions. He didn't always want to, especially after a tough loss in which he'd failed to get on the scoreboard. It came with the territory, though, so Ryder did it. After all, nobody

5

liked a sore loser.

Some of the things expected of him, Ryder enjoyed, such as contributing his favorite recipe—pizza burgers— to the Generals Foundation cookbook, or visiting sick kids in the hospital. He had no reason to complain about those, especially since both were for a good cause.

So was the bachelor auction, but Ryder still considered it torture. Even though he'd never before wished he was married, now Ryder did. Or if not married, at least seriously dating someone. If he were, he'd get a pass on this dreaded event.

Instead, he sat on a stage, dressed in his best suit and tie, and prepared to be paraded in front of the audience so that women could bid on him. Or rather, they could bid on a date with him. That was the most Ryder agreed to. One date, for the highest bidder. A drink and dinner, perhaps even dessert if things went sort of well. But nothing beyond that. No way. He was a hockey player, for goodness sake, not a gigolo or an escort. Besides, he had bigger priorities, like winning a Stanley Cup.

"This is going to be great," his teammate, Casey Deanult, said from the seat next to Ryder. "Lots of women out here, and probably plenty of hot ones."

If they're so hot, why are they so desperate? Ryder wondered, then felt a little guilty. It was a charity event, after all, so maybe their intentions were good. It wasn't fair to judge all of the women in attendance as either cheap or desperate. "Good. They can bid on you," he said to Casey.

"I hope so. The more the merrier." Casey grinned. "As I like to say, the only thing better than one smoking hot chick is two smoking hot chicks. Or maybe three," he added with a shrug of his shoulders. "I don't like to discriminate."

Ryder grimaced at the crude implications of Casey's remark. No doubt about it, his teammate was a horn dog of the worst kind. He knew he wasn't the only guy on the team that worried Casey would someday get himself into trouble with his womanizing ways, but what could they do about it? Casey showed up to work every day and gave the team his best.

"Then hopefully they're all here for you and you can have an orgy," Ryder muttered under his breath. "I don't want anything to do with this whole charade." Except it was for charity, so he couldn't exactly say no. Instead, the best Ryder could hope for was that whoever bid on him—assuming anyone did—turned out to be a nice, respectable woman who'd done so only to further the charitable cause, and not because she looked to score with a professional athlete.

"Oh, lighten up, Carrigan," Casey said. "It's all in fun. Hot women and charity. And as a bonus, we even get the babe from channel twelve covering the event." He whistled softly under his breath. "Man, I'd love to tap that."

"Sheesh, Denault, are you ever not an ass?" Ryder asked. "You might as well get over that fantasy. She's a professional here to do her job. Not pay money to spend an hour with you." He couldn't deny, though, that the local news anchor sent to report on the event for her network was one beautiful woman.

***

Jessica Rowan wished she could be any place else but where she was, forced to cover a celebrity bachelor auction for San Antonio's ABC affiliate. It wasn't that she didn't believe in the cause—suicide prevention and awareness—she just wasn't convinced the event was the best way to support said cause. Win a date with a professional hockey player to help prevent suicide? Jessica had a hard time seeing the connection.

She'd agreed to cover the event because Charlenes Simmons, who headed the Generals Charity Foundation, was one of her closest friends, and because her boss at the station, who'd lost a teenager to suicide, insisted channel twelve should be there. None of the other local news stations thought the auction was worth covering, so it was Jessica's gig, and hers alone. Since that wasn't anything to sneeze at in the echelon of television news reporting, Jessica was determined to make it work for her, even if she did think the whole thing was rather silly.

After interviewing Matt Johnson, who was the son of the Generals owner and the team's marketing director, and Char, it was time to move on to the big stars. The Generals players. Since the team captain and marquee player, Colton Tremblay, had recently announced his engagement, he wasn't participating in the auction. Neither was Alex Gray, one of the Generals Alternate Captains, who was married with a young son. That left the team's other Alternate Captain, left winger Ryder Carrigan, to be the first player Jessica spoke to.

"Ryder Carrigan finished the season fourth in points among all Generals players, and looks forward to building on that success in his second season in San Antonio," Jessica said. "But before that can happen, he has to survive tonight's bachelor auction." She strived for a dramatic tone and hoped it didn't sound completely over the top or stupid.

"Ryder, can you tell us what you're looking forward to the most about tonight's event?" As she thrust the microphone at him, Jessica was struck with two thoughts. The first was that he had the prettiest eyes of anyone she'd ever seen. Eyes she could easily get lost in.

The second was that Ryder Carrigan looked like he'd rather be any place else at that moment, which Jess could certainly relate to.

***

What was he looking forward to most? How about nothing? No, that wouldn't be an acceptable answer. For this whole dreaded event to be over? That would be the honest answer, but probably not one Ryder wanted broadcast on the evening news. Pushing the microphone away from his face wasn't a good option, either. That would be a rude, asshole-ish thing to do. The reporter was only doing her job.

"Helping to raise awareness for an important cause," Ryder said. "I think in our brief time in this city, the Generals franchise has proven to have a strong commitment to charity, and this is another way for us to show that commitment. And who knows, maybe we'll have a little fun in the process." He didn't believe that, but hopefully it sounded good.

The news anchor nodded. "When the idea of the bachelor auction was first announced, were you excited to volunteer your services?"

His services? Ryder cringed inwardly. It did make him sound like a damn escort. Is that really what she thought, or was it simply an unfortunate choice of words? He hoped for the latter, because if they had to have this event, he at least wanted it to earn some halfway decent news coverage for the right reasons.

"I wouldn't say excited, exactly," Ryder answered after a second. "I think my teammates will tell you I'm not much into celebrity and all of that. I'm more of a homebody," he said, "so this isn't really my kind of thing. But I'm proud to be considered one of the leaders on our team, and I'm a single guy, so it kind of goes with the territory." He shrugged. "I don't mind doing this because it's such a worthy cause. That's really what it's about for me."

"That's it, just the charity?" The news anchor smiled, her brown eyes twinkling. "You aren't secretly hoping to find your soulmate tonight?"

"No, ma'am, I'm not." Ryder returned her smile. "You never know, though. I'm sure stranger things have happened."

Their eyes locked for a second before the reporter turned away from Ryder to face her cameraman again. "Well, there you have it. Ryder Carrigan may not be looking for love, but he's not opposed to finding it. And maybe it will happen right here, tonight."

CHAPTER TWO

What the heck? That wasn't what he'd said at all. Nothing like having his words completely twisted. There was nothing Ryder could do to correct it, however, as Jessica Rowan had already moved on along with her cameraman, to try get good sound bites from the rest of the guys. Ryder sat back down, making a mental note to be more careful with his words next time. Not that it would make any difference. People always liked to put their own interpretation on things.

He glanced at his watch. Only five minutes to go until the dreaded event started, but the sooner it started, the sooner it would be over. And fortunately, the set-up was a silent auction format, which meant he wouldn't be subjected to a loud and raucous scream fest. No, all he had to do was walk back and forth across the stage while the event's hosts—the Generals in-game arena announcer, Grant Dahlstrom, and the reporter from channel twelve—gave their vital stats to everyone in the audience. That would be plenty embarrassing enough, but at least none of the guys would never know how money each of them fetched.

For that, Ryder was grateful. The Generals had a close-knit locker room, but a playful and competitive one, too, and no doubt the guy that garnered the least interest at the auction was sure to face some good-natured ribbing. At least the silent bidding would prevent that.

The lights dimmed, and the co-hosts stepped forward on the stage. "Ladies and Gentlemen, welcome to the First Annual San Antonio Generals Charity Foundation Bachelor Auction! I'm the voice of the Generals, Grant Dahlstrom, and with me tonight is the very lovely Jessica Rowan from KSAT channel twelve, and do we have a show for you." He paused to allow for applause. "In just a few minutes, you'll be introduced to fifteen eligible bachelors from your San Antonio Generals, and you'll be given an opportunity to win a date with one of them. Or more, I suppose, if your checkbook allows for it," the emcee added. Predictably, the audience laughed.

Perfect, Ryder thought. *Casey can have his orgy.*

"Jessica, before we get started, why don't you tell everyone a little bit about why we're here, and the importance of tonight's event?" Grant suggested.

"Thank you, Grant, and thank you, everyone for being here. Tonight's bachelor auction benefits the Texas Youth Suicide Prevention Project, which is a cause that is near and dear to all our hearts at channel twelve, because as most of you know, our news director, Anthony Madsen, recently lost his son to suicide..."

As Ryder listened to her remarks, he relaxed. Okay, maybe he still hated public showcases like this, but being reminded, in a very human way, of why they were doing this, helped. He didn't know Tony Madsen in person, and never met his son TJ, but this was real. It might be too late to help TJ, but if the money raised tonight brought awareness to the cause, and maybe, in some way, helped someone else like TJ Madsen, then it was all worth it. Who knows, maybe he'd even have a reasonably pleasant time with whomever bid on him.

If Ryder was uncomfortable with the whole idea of the auction, his teammate, Jonathan Ackerman, looked even more so as, by way of the alphabet, he got to be the first bachelor paraded across the stage. Ryder felt for Jon. The kid was barely old enough to legally drink in the United States and came over from his native Sweden to play in the NHL. And he had to be subjected to this? He was a good sport, though, waving to the audience as he made his walk across the stage.

And then it was Ryder's turn.

"An alternate captain for the Generals, left wing Ryder Carrigan stands six feet one, and hails from Victoria, British Columbia," Grant announced, as if Ryder's height and hometown were the two most important things about him.

"Victoria. I believe that's where the reigning Conn Smythe winner, and captain of the Stanley Cup Champions, hails from," Jessica said. "Perhaps this coming season, Ryder can help bring the Cup down I-35 from Dallas to San Antonio."

Great. Nothing like putting pressure on a guy. Ryder was a fan of the Dallas Stars' captain, having grown up in the same town and played youth hockey with him. He'd never be a superstar like his hometown friend was, and Ryder was okay with that. Except for one thing. Jamie had his name on the Stanley Cup, and that was what Ryder coveted most of all.

He waved, turned, and made his walk back to his seat as Grant and Jessica continued their commentary about Ryder's favorite food and his favorite TV show, in case these things might cause some woman in attendance to decide she just had to meet him. And then, thankfully, it was all done. All Ryder had to do was watch the other guys preen and prance. Then they'd eat dinner, and after that, he'd learn who bid on him. Whew. Not so bad. As long as the date didn't turn out to be a disaster.

***

Once all of the eligible bachelors were introduced, and had made their walk across the stage, the silent bidding opened, which allowed Jessica a much-needed break from her reporting and co-host duties. She made her way to the cash bar, where she got a glass of white wine from a local Texas winery.

"You're doing a great job so far, Jess," a woman said, coming up beside her. It was Char. "Thanks again for agreeing to do this."

"No problem." Between her friendship with Char and her boss's personal connection to the cause, it wasn't something she could really say no to. Jessica took a sip of wine. "At least the toughest part is over now," she said, referring the player interviews and introductions. "As long as I don't flub somebody's name announcing the winners, the rest should be pretty smooth sailing."

"Yeah, and I think we're going to have some high bid amounts," Char said. "I stole a glance at the auction table on my way over here, and it was already busy."

"Wow. That's great."

Char nodded. "Yep. Lots of money for a good cause. I can't say I'm surprised, though, because this is a pretty sexy group of bachelors we've got."

"That it is," Jessica agreed. "Are you bidding?" she asked her friend. Even though they'd been in college at UT San Antonio at the same time, Char was older than Jessica by about ten years, having gone back to college after a divorce. She now approached her fortieth birthday, and even though it was still several months away, Jessica knew her friend dreaded the milestone—and being single.

"Can't. I work for the team, remember?" Char shrugged and took a drink. "You can, though," she added with a conspiratorial wink.

"Ha ha. As if."

"Why not? You've been saying for the past year that you want to find a nice guy and settle down," Char reminded her.

It was true. The closer she got to thirty, the more Jessica thought about it. She'd spent the past six plus years focusing on her career, working her way up from occasional weekend reporter to weeknight news anchor, and she loved the work. But lately, more and more, she found herself wanting more. "Yes, settle down," Jessica said. "With a guy who's here, not on the road all the time."

"They're not traveling all the time. Usually it's only a few days at a time," Char said.

"If you say so." Jessica wasn't in the mood to argue. "Either way, the professional athlete thing isn't my scene," she said. "Even if they are nice guys." And she had to admit, they definitely seemed to be. And she sure couldn't deny that they were easy on the eyes.

"Fine. I was only kidding, anyway. I don't expect you to bid," Char said. "If you were, though, who'd be your first choice?"

The question was all in fun, but Jessica gave it consideration before answering. "I don't know. I think I'd have to go with Ryder. He seems pretty down-to-earth, not full of himself," she said. "And I like his smile."

Char nodded. "Good choice. From what I know of him, Ryder's a stand up guy. Anyway, I should go mingle. I'll catch you after the auction?"

"Sure," Jessica said. "I want to grab a bite and make the rounds, anyway, before the bidding ends and we have to announce the winners."

After saying goodbye to Char, Jessica went to get some finger food and stopped to chat with her boss, who praised the job she was doing so far, which she appreciated. No doubt this was a difficult night for Tony and his whole family. She made small talk with various attendees over the course of the next hour, and soon it was time to take the stage with Grant again to announce the winners.

"Wow, the time sure passed quickly, didn't it?" Grant asked. "I hear we've raised quite a bit of money here tonight, and I bet the guys here on the stage behind me want to know who bid on them." After the cheers quieted down, he continued. "First up is Jonathan Ackerman, and the lucky winner of a date with the young Generals center is..." Grant paused dramatically as he looked at the list in his hand. "Beth Wilcox.

Congratulations, Beth. Come up to the stage when we're all done tonight, and you can meet Jon and make plans for your date." He turned to Jessica. "Do you want to announce the next winner?"

"I sure will," Jessica said. "Our next lucky winner gets a date with the Generals winger and alternate captain, Ryder Carrigan. And she is..." As cheesy as it was, Jessica did the dramatic pause, too, as if this were a Hollywood awards show, before glancing down at the winner's list.

Then she froze.

"Jessica, are you okay?" Grant asked. "Maybe I should announce the winner." He looked at the paper in his hand and let out a chuckle. "Okay, that explains why my co-host is a little flustered. It seems that the winner of a date with Ryder is our very own Jessica Rowan."

MICHELE SHRIVER

CHAPTER THREE

The crowd whooped and hollered, leaving Jessica mortified. There was only one person who could be responsible for this, and Jessica would deal with her soon enough. First, though, she had a job to do, and a little face to save. "Hey, I can't let everyone else here have all the fun, can I? This is a great group of bachelors, and such a worthy cause."

"That it is," Grant agreed. "Okay, let's keep going. Next up is Casey Deanult. In his short time in San Antonio, the Generals center has developed quite a reputation as a ladies man. Can he be tamed? One lucky lady gets the opportunity, and her name is Alicia Warner."

Whew. The embarrassment passed. Jessica owed Grant a major thank you for not dwelling on her surprise appearance on the winners' list and quickly moving on to the next announcement. She was equally grateful that the audience seemed to have a short attention span. They wanted to hear the names of all of the winners, not focus only on one, and Jessica was happy to oblige them.

It was over soon enough, and the winners were told they should find their bachelor to work out the arrangements of their date. Jessica was interested in finding someone, too, and it wasn't Ryder Carrigan. Fortunately, she didn't have to look very hard.

Char stood off to the right of the stage, sporting an amused smirk.

"I could kill you," Jessica hissed as she approached.

"You could, yes, but you'd get arrested."

"My brother's a lawyer," Jessica answered. "I'm sure he could get me off on some sort of justification defense"

Char's smile faded slightly, but she didn't apologize. "Come on, Jess. What happened to your sense of humor?"

"Nothing," she said through clenched teeth. "I just don't find this stunt particularly amusing. What were you thinking, Char?"

Her friend shrugged nonchalantly. "I was thinking I had money to spend, but I couldn't bid for myself. So I thought I'd treat my best friend to an evening out with a nice, handsome man," Char explained. "One you said yourself you were interested in."

"What? I said nothing of the sort," Jessica protested. Talk about twisting words. "I only said that if I were to pick one of the guys, it would probably be Ryder. That's it. I never said I was interested in dating him." She shook her head. Char was unbelievable.

"Semantics," Char offered with a roll of her eyes. "It was all in fun, but fine... if that's really the way you feel about it, then cancel the date," she said. "You've got your chance right now, because here comes Ryder."

"What?" Jessica turned around, and sure enough, he was headed in her direction,

"Ms. Rowan." He extended a hand.

He had manners, for sure, and she shook his hand. "You can call me Jessica."

"Sure, okay." He nodded. "So, I guess you had the highest bid. I have to admit, I was pretty surprised to hear your name announced."

Not half as surprised as I was. "Yeah, about that... I didn't actually bid on you," Jessica said. She jerked a thumb over her shoulder in Char's direction. "My friend here thought it would be fun to bid for me." Best to make it clear right away that this was all Char's doing, and not Jessica's own wish.

***

Ryder was surprised, but pleasantly so, to learn the news anchor won the bidding war for a date with him. Not so much because he liked to stay under the radar— though he did—but because he didn't think the event's co-host would participate in the bidding. He couldn't deny he was pleased, though. She may have misconstrued his words a little, but she was a beautiful woman, and carried herself with a certain class and professionalism. It would be nice to get to know her better.

He found her after the auction ended chatting with the director of the team's charity foundation, who'd put together the whole event. As soon as he approached, though, things went in a different direction than Ryder expected. He thought Jessica would be pleased to see him, and they'd make arrangements to go for dinner. He even had a few upscale restaurants in mind. Before he could suggest them, Jessica informed him she hadn't been the one to bid on him, leaving Ryder at a temporary loss for words.

"Oh, um, well..." He searched for a way to make a graceful exit. Sure, he was a little disappointed, but he wasn't going to dwell on it. And Ryder certainly wasn't going to let her know he was disappointed. He was a professional athlete. He made five million dollars a year. He didn't need a damn bachelor auction to find a date. "So you're saying you want to cancel, then? Just give the money to the charity and call it a night?" Ryder could live with that, even if it wasn't his first choice.

"I didn't say that," Jessica answered. "Only that I wasn't the one who made the bid."

"That would be me." The other woman gave Ryder a smile. "Charlene Simmons. I run the charity foundation."

"Yes, of course. Thanks for putting this together."

"Thanks for participating."

It's not like I had much choice. Ryder shrugged. "It's part of the job, and I don't really mind," he said. "So you're the one who actually bid money to go on a date with me?"

Charlene nodded. "Yes, but I did it on Jess's behalf. I'm not allowed to participate, and I have no stake in this, other than raising money. I'll leave it up to the two of you how you want to handle it. I won't be heartbroken either way, because the money went to the cause."

So Jessica's friend was essentially trying to play matchmaker. That's what it sounded like to Ryder. He didn't mind, exactly, but Jessica didn't seem at all enthused, and he saw little point in wasting time on a date she wanted no part of. "Okay, then..." he turned back to Jessica. "Your call. What do you want to do?" Maybe he was putting her on the spot, but he did need an answer. He expected it to be a no, and then it would all be over. And maybe that was for the best.

"I think we should put my friend's money to good use," Jessica said after a minute. "So what did you have in mind? Dinner? A movie?"

"Either's fine. Or..." Ryder paused. Jessica surprised him by actually agreeing to the date, and now he wanted to do something different, unexpected. Definitely not the fallback dinner and a movie. Besides, was anything good playing? Probably not, and it was hard to get to know somebody in a movie. No, he needed something better. "Do you like jazz?"

"Hmm?"

"Jazz music. The jazz festival is this weekend in Travis Park," Ryder said. "I thought maybe we could do that. It's my last free weekend before we leave for training camp in El Paso."

"Oh, sure. That sounds fun," Jessica said. "I do like jazz, and I have the weekend off. Should I meet you there?"

After a second, Ryder nodded. Sure, he could pick her up. But this was an arranged date, after all. Meeting there would probably be best. That way nobody was bound to anything. "Sure. Maybe Saturday around one, at the festival entrance?"

"That works." Jessica smiled, and the twinkle returned to her brown eyes. "One o'clock Saturday. It's a date."

"Yes. I guess it is. I'll see you then," Ryder said. He knew he'd look forward to it. The question was, would Jessica? It made things a little awkward knowing she hadn't been the one to bid, but hey… she'd agreed to the date, even when he'd offered her the chance to back out. That had to count for something.

***

"What the heck did I just do?" Jessica mused out loud after Ryder left to rejoin some of his teammates.

"Um, agreed to a date with a sexy hockey player," Char said, once again sporting the all-too-familiar smirk.

"The question was intended rhetorically," Jessica muttered. "And do you have to look so damn pleased with yourself?"

"Actually, yes." Char chuckled. "Because tonight has gone better than I could have expected. All of the bachelors were bid on, the Foundation raised a boatload of money, and you're about to go on a date with Ryder."

"An arranged date," Jessica said. "One that neither one of us is actually interested in."

"Bullshit," Char said. "Didn't you see the look on his face when he found out you weren't the one that bid? The guy was seriously bummed, Jess."

She thought about that, had to admit her friend was right. Ryder had looked disappointed when he learned it was actually Char who'd done the bidding. It was one of the reasons why Jessica had decided to accept the date, even when he graciously gave her the chance to bow out. "It was probably just a blow to his ego."

Char rolled her eyes. "I don't believe that, and neither do you. I think Ryder is very much looking forward to Saturday," she declared. "And more importantly, so are you."

"If you say so." Jessica didn't intend to give Char the satisfaction of knowing she was right. "At least I like jazz, so hopefully it will be a tolerable afternoon. If not, I still might kill you."

"In that case, I'm not too worried," Char said with a laugh. "Come on, let me buy you drink. Maybe you'll lighten up a little bit."

MICHELE SHRIVER

CHAPTER FOUR

Being fairly new to San Antonio, Ryder had never been to the jazz festival, but he'd heard good things about it. Hopefully the positive word of mouth boded well for the afternoon with Jessica. Assuming she showed up. Part of him wondered if she might stand him up. After all, she had been roped into the date by her friend.

Ryder got to the park entrance a few minutes before one and waited outside for her, pleased that he could do so anonymously. There was something to be said for playing for an expansion team in a non-traditional hockey city. In his cargo shorts, golf shirt, and Wayfarer shades, Ryder blended in and wasn't likely to be recognized. No, his date, who graced the six and ten o'clock newscasts five nights a week, was probably the more famous one, or at least more recognizable.

As he pondered that, Ryder saw Jessica approaching. She wore denim Capri length pants and a pink shirt, and her blond hair fell loosely past her shoulders. No doubt about it, her looks hadn't hindered her chances of getting a job in television, even if it was shallow to think that. Ryder waved her over. "Hi, Jessica."

"Hi." She greeted him with a sunny smile. "Pretty nice day, huh?"

"Not too bad." The Texas heat still took some getting used to, especially compared to the mild climate in British Columbia, but the humidity was low and all indications were it would be a pleasant afternoon, at least in terms of the weather. "Shall we go inside?"

"Sure. I've been looking forward to this."

"You have?" That was nice to hear, considering how the date came about.

"Yeah, one of the bands was featured on our newscast last night, so I'm anxious to hear them."

They approached the festival entrance, and Ryder realized admission was free. "I hope you don't think I'm a cheapskate," he joked

"Nah." Jessica chuckled. "But you can buy lunch to dispel any doubt."

"Consider it done," he said, appreciating that she had a sense of humor. "You've already paid enough for the chance to spend a day with me. Or rather, your friend did."

"Money well spent," Jessica said, though the statement left room for doubt whether it was because of him or the charitable cause the auction had benefitted.

"Do you want to get food right away?" Ryder asked. "What time does the band you want to hear play?"

"Not until three. Lunch sounds good."

They made their way over to the food vendors and

checked out the options before settling on tacos. Ryder bought them each a beer and they found a shady area to sit and eat. He wished he'd thought to bring a couple of chairs, or at least a blanket, but Jessica didn't seem to mind sitting in the grass.

"You may have to help me up, though," she joked.

"That's assuming I can get up myself," Ryder countered. "My body took some wear and tear over the season." Then he'd spent part of the summer coaching at the Young Generals hockey camp. As a result, training camp started in a few days and he felt as if he hadn't had much break at all.

"Are you anxious for the new season to start?"

"Yes," Ryder answered without hesitation. "We didn't like the way the last one ended." Sure, the team qualified for the playoffs, which was impressive for an expansion team, but the first round loss left them all hungry for more. Especially Ryder, who coveted his name on the Stanley Cup more than anything. "Don't take this the wrong way, but I'm happy to be done with the community stuff and be able to get back on the ice. That's where I'm comfortable. I don't much care for the spotlight."

Jessica nodded as she took a bite of lunch. "Yeah, I got that impression the other night. You didn't look as if you really wanted to be at that auction."

"You noticed, huh?" Ryder took a drink of beer and stretched his legs out. "No, not real bad," he admitted. "But it worked out okay. I get to spend the afternoon with you."

***

Jessica felt the warmth rise to her cheeks. "Oh, well..." She wasn't sure what to say, which was silly. She'd gotten compliments from men before, plenty of them. Some were welcome, others not. None of them had been superstar athletes, though. Jessica suspected Ryder might argue with the whole superstar designation, and that made him even more attractive. "It's worked out pretty well for me, too."

"Yeah?" Ryder raised an eyebrow. "It didn't exactly look like you thought so the other night," he said. "You seemed pretty upset with your friend."

"I was," Jessica admitted. In hindsight, her reaction had probably been a little harsh. There were far worse ways to spend a Saturday afternoon than attending a jazz festival with an NHL player who was very easy on the eyes and also seemed to be a genuinely nice guy. "I don't like being blindsided or embarrassed, and I was both when I saw my name on that card and was expected to read it out loud."

"You've been a good sport about it," Ryder said. "We didn't have to do this. The money we raised was what mattered."

"Definitely," Jessica said. "But it seemed silly to back out." She finished her taco and washed it down with a swallow of beer. "I'm enjoying getting to know you." She wanted to make sure he understood that.

"Me too," Ryder said. "So how'd you end up hosting the auction? Something about the cause being important to your boss?"

Jessica nodded. "Yes, our station manager lost his seventeen-year-old son to suicide last year," she explained. "TJ was gay, and subjected to bullying, as a result. I guess it got to be too much for him." Jessica closed her eyes, trying to reconcile the bright, happy eleven-year-old TJ Madsen she'd met when she first began working at channel twelve with the despondent teen who'd believed all hope was lost.

"Wow." Ryder exhaled. "That's heartbreaking. People can be so cruel." He shook his head. "I guess I was fortunate. I was a boy growing up in Canada, and my folks put me in skates pretty much as soon as I could walk. And even though I'll never be a big name NHL star, I'm blessed to have the ability to play a game I love and make money doing it. Even if I don't like the celebrity part of my job, being able to do things to help others, like this event and some of the others I've been involved in, both here and when I played for the Rangers, make me feel like maybe my job is sort of important," he said. "I mean, it's mainly entertainment, but we can do some good things, too, and maybe even make a difference."

"You can, absolutely," Jessica said. Even if she was somewhat jaded in her world view—she blamed reporting the news, which wasn't usually positive—she had to appreciate his words. Ryder got it. He understood. And it made her like him even more. "You've already done a lot for this community."

"Your friend, our foundation director, she's responsible for that," Ryder said.

"No doubt. Char's tireless in what she does."

"So you're not too mad at her, then, for setting this up?"

"Nah." Jessica shook her head. "So far, it's working out pretty well."

"Just 'pretty well?'" Ryder asked. "I don't know whether I should be offended by your low expectations or challenged to do better."

Jessica cocked her head to the side as she contemplated that. He was cute, no doubt about it, and said all the right things. And seemed sincere as he said them. She should probably be more impressed. "Challenged," she said after a slight hesitation. "When in doubt, always take the challenge."

"Okay, then," Ryder said with a laugh. "Challenge accepted." He pulled himself up off the ground before extending a hand to help Jessica up. "Let's walk around a bit before the band starts."

***

So far, so good. Jessica accepted his help in getting up from the grass, then kept her hand linked with Ryder's as they strolled the park. The soft, soothing sounds of jazz played in the background, but this apparently wasn't the band Jessica wanted most to hear, so Ryder was content to walk around and take in the other sights.

They stopped at a craft booth, where Jessica seemed drawn to the pretty, multi-colored woven bracelets, so Ryder brought her one.

"You didn't have to do that," she said, as he helped her fasten it on her wrist.

"No, but I got off fairly easy on the cost of admission," he reminded her. Besides, the small gesture made her smile, and he liked her smile. They continued their stroll, pausing occasionally to look at the various crafts. This time, when Jessica found a piece of Aztec pottery she liked, Ryder let her buy it herself, but offered to carry the bag.

As they wandered back to the music stage to try to get a good spot to watch the next band, they ran into Ryder's teammate, Trevor Collison, with his girlfriend Danielle, and their daughter, Kaylen, and he was surprised to learn that Jessica knew Danielle.

"My brother's a lawyer, and Dani used to be a legal secretary at his firm," Jessica explained, when Ryder questioned the connection.

"And I will be again," Dani said. "I'm just taking an extended leave while Kaylen recovers. I'll be back, though."

Ryder nodded, wanting to believe her. Trevor and Dani's daughter had undergone a bone marrow transplant in the spring, and Trevor had been the donor. It caused him to miss the playoffs, which undoubtedly hurt the team's chances of advancing, but all of the guys had rallied to support him. Family was more important, and seeing Kaylen walking around now, no longer confined to a wheelchair, gave Ryder hope. So far, good. The transplant took, and Kaylen seemed to be gaining strength every day. Trevor's new four-year contract with the team made certain that Dani shouldn't have to work any more, but at the same time, he understood that her getting back to her job would be a sign that Kaylen was better and things were returning to normal. And he wanted that for Trevor and his family more than anything.

"I know that's what Mike and Ellis want to see," Jessica said. "You'll always have a job there if you want one."

"Are you guys hanging around for a while?" Ryder asked Trevor. "Jessica knows the next band and wants to hear them, so I can get us some drinks," he suggested.

"Sure," Trevor said. "Special Kay is feeling good, so I think we'll stay a little longer, right, baby?"

"Yeah, at least for a while," Dani agreed. "Thanks, Ryder."

"No problem." He gave Jessica's hand a squeeze. "Why don't you find us a good place to hear the band, and I'll be back in a few?"

"Sure, that sounds good," said.

"I'll come with you," Trevor said. "To help you carry them." He kissed Dani's cheek. "We'll be right back."

Great, Ryder thought as Trevor fell into step beside him. *Time to be grilled about my date.*

CHAPTER FIVE

It was all Jessica could do not to laugh when Trevor decided to accompany Ryder to get drinks for them, leaving her with Dani and Kaylen. "That wasn't exactly subtle, was it?"

Dani did laugh. "Not at all. I've got to admit, we've been a little curious how the dates from the auction would play out."

"We?" Jessica asked, as located seats with a decent view of the stage and sat down. "Who's we? You and Trevor?"

"Oh, sorry. Yes, Trevor and me," Dani said. "As well as the other WAGs who were fortunate to be amused observers the other night."

WAGs. The wives and girlfriends of the athletes. Jessica knew enough about sports to be familiar with the terminology, even if she didn't care for it. "Amused, huh?"

"Very much so. We kept a running commentary going the whole time," Dani said. "Casey's a player, so it was probably a fantasy come true for him. Ryder, on the other hand, we figured just wanted it to all be over with, and the sooner the better."

Jessica nodded. "I got that same impression when I interviewed him before the auction started."

"Yet you bid on him, anyway," Dani said. "That's very interesting."

"Oh, no, I didn't bid. Char was responsible for that," Jessica explained. Dani knew Char as well, thanks to the team's efforts to help her out during her daughter's illness.

"Really?" Dani's expression broke out in a grin. "Now this I can totally see."

"Yeah, typical Char. I kind of wanted to kill her."

"Yet here you are... with Ryder."

"Yeah, here I am." Jessica watched the musicians setting up on the stage. "With Ryder..."

"You don't sound terribly thrilled about that," Dani observed. "What's the matter? Are you not having a good time?"

"Actually, I'm having a great time," Jessica admitted. "He's a gentleman. He has a sense of humor, and doesn't take himself too seriously. And he's definitely not bad to look at."

"Maybe I'm missing something, but those all seem to be good qualities in a date."

"They are, for sure," Jessica agreed.

"So what's the problem, exactly?" Dani frowned. "Are you seeing someone else? Or not interested in a relationship at all?"

Jessica shook her head. "No on both counts. I'm very much single, and open to a relationship. In fact, I'm getting tired of being alone. Char knows that, and that's why she set this up." She sighed. "As attractive as

Ryder is, this isn't the kind of relationship I'm interested in. I want someone I can settle down with. Someone I can count on to be around. Not someone who's on the road half the time." She turned to look at Dani. "How do you do it?"

"That's a good question. I don't know. The season was almost over before Trev and I found our way back to each other," Dani said. "I guess we're about to find out. It scares me a little, but we'll figure it out. We'll be okay."

She sounded confident, and Jessica wanted it for her. "I'm sure you will. You guys have a history together. That makes a difference."

***

"To help me carry them, huh?" Okay, it wouldn't be easy to juggle drinks for five people, but Ryder was wise to Trevor's ulterior motive.

"Well, you know..." Trevor gave a sheepish smile as they got in line at the beverage stand.

"Yeah."

"So, since we're here anyway, how are things going?"

"Good." Ryder didn't even have to think about it. "Real good. I like Jessica. I still think the auction idea was silly, but that's beside the point. I have no idea how the other guys' dates are going, but I think I fared pretty well in the whole process." It was way too soon to tell where things were headed with Jessica, but Ryder was happy to have the chance to spend an afternoon with her.

"I think Casey was a little put off when she didn't

bid on him," Trevor said, causing Ryder to roll his eyes.

"Naturally, because Casey thinks all women should be after him."

"Of course." Trevor laughed. "I wonder if anyone will ever tame him."

"Who knows? Maya sure tamed Colton pretty fast," Ryder said, referring to their team captain who'd come to San Antonio after a trade from Montreal with quite a reputation of his own as a womanizer and a playboy. Now he was happily engaged to a local sports writer and planning a wedding after the new season ended—which they all hoped was not until sometime in June. Preferably in late June. Maybe after the Stanley Cup parade. A guy had to have dreams, and that was Ryder's.

"That she did," Trevor said. "And then look at Dani and me."

"Oh?" Ryder arched his brows. "Is there something you haven't told any of us yet?"

"Nah." Trevor shook his head. "I mean, it's on the radar for sure. Now that I got her back, I can't imagine being with anyone besides Dani. But things are still pretty new this time around, and our focus is on Kaylen right now."

"As it should be." It had turned into the feel good story of the league. The guy who battled back from drug addiction, trying to resurrect his career with an expansion team, and he reconnects with the first woman he ever loved, then gets to save the life of the daughter he never knew they had. It was hard to script things better than that. "She looks good, Trev."

He nodded. "She feels good, too. She'll be plenty tired after today, but she wanted to come, and being outside is good for her."

"Glad to hear it." Ryder made his way to to front of the concession line and ordered a couple beers for him and Jessica. "What about you?" he asked Trevor.

"The same, and a water for Kaylen."

"Got it." Ryder got his wallet out and paid for all of them.

"Wow, you're Mr. Generous today," Trevor teased. "This date must be going well."

"Oh, funny man." Ryder handed Trevor two of the beers and the water and they made their way back over to the stage. Jessica and Dani had found good seats, so they would have no problem seeing or hearing the band.

"Here you go," he said, giving Jessica her drink before sitting down beside her.

"Thanks. And good timing. They're just about to start."

***

The band lived up to Jessica's expectations, and she thoroughly enjoyed their music. It appeared that Ryder did, too, since they stayed for the entire performance. Trevor and Dani left after the first set, stating their daughter was tired, and Jessica didn't doubt it. The little girl had been through a lot. Ryder, though, never appeared bored or expressed a desire to leave.

"Good show," he said as the last set concluded. "I liked them."

"Classic New Orleans jazz. There's nothing better."

"If you say so. I've never been to New Orleans."

"You haven't?" Jessica had a hard time keeping the surprise from her voice, even if it really wasn't a shocking declaration.

Ryder shook his head. "Nope. Hey, I'm from Canada, remember?"

"True enough. And I've never been there." Jessica laughed.

"Never been to Canada?" Ryder frowned. "Then perhaps it's time to change that. You should travel to one of our road games," he suggested.

Following the team on the road? Did he mean as a groupie, or WAG? Or had he simply meant as a spectator? "Maybe I'll get the chance to someday," Jessica said as they got up from their seats and left the stage area. "And you should visit New Orleans."

"I want to, for sure," Ryder said. "Do you want to look around some more, or can I walk you to your car?"

Ah, the dreaded is the date over, or not, moment. Jessica both loved and hated dating. Loved it, because career woman be damned, she'd be lying if she said she didn't want to find her soul mate and start a family, and hated it, because, well, hello awkwardness. Like now. How was she supposed to respond to Ryder's question? The truth was, she was tired. It was a warm day. She'd had a good time, but was also ready to go home. But if she said that, would he be put off? Yeah. She hated dating.

"Would you be offended if I said the latter?" Jessica asked. "I've had a good time, but I work on Monday, and Sundays are kind of my only 'me day,' if you know what I mean." Was she rambling too much?

"I get it," Ryder said with a casual smile. "I leave for El Paso early on Monday, so we're cool. I'll just take you to your car."

She wanted to tell him he didn't even have to do that, but Jessica appreciated the gesture. Ryder was a gentleman, for sure. They walked the short two blocks to where she'd parked, and Jessica unlocked her Mini with her key fob. "This is me."

Ryder nodded. "Cute car."

"Thanks. I always wanted one, even though my mom keeps telling me it'll have to go if I ever have kids." Now what did she go and say that for?

"Maybe, maybe not," Ryder said with a shrug. "Anyway, thanks for agreeing to the date, in spite of the circumstances."

"My pleasure," Jessica said. "I really did have a nice time."

"I'm glad." He jammed his hands in his pockets. "So, um..."

Hello, awkwardness! "Yes?"

"I had a good time, too," Ryder said. "In case you wanted to do it again..."

Yes, this was beyond awkward, but he was so darn cute when he was being shy and uncertain. Was it all an act? Jessica hated to be cynical. "I could probably be persuaded." She smiled. "You can call me at the station when you get back from El Paso, if you're interested."

MICHELE SHRIVER

CHAPTER SIX

The second San Antonio Generals Training Camp differed quite a bit from the first, and not only because it was held in a different city. The previous year had been filled with uncertainty. There was excitement, of course, about being the league's newest franchise, but unfamiliarity, too. Most of the guys barely knew each other, having all come from different teams.

On the first day of training camp the year before, Ryder was selected as an alternate captain. He didn't know why the coaching staff chose him. He hadn't worn a letter since his days in the American Hockey League. It was an honor, though, and he'd vowed that day to make his teammates proud.

A year later, that remained his goal, as he stood with Captain Colton Tremblay, and Alex Gray, the other alternate captain, to address the guys in the locker room. Sixty guys, as young as eighteen and as old as thirty six—their veteran defenseman Seth Rollins—made up the training camp roster. Twenty three of them would open the season on the Generals roster, while another twenty six would ultimately begin the regular season in El Paso, playing for the AHL affiliate Aztecs. The remainder would return to their junior leagues or college.

Or in the case of the franchise's newest draft pick, high school. The kid had just turned eighteen two weeks before, narrowly making him eligible for this draft class, and he'd earned a camp invite mainly just so he could get a taste of what an NHL training camp was like, even though he was likely to spend at least two years at the University of New Hampshire, where he'd committed to play college hockey. After he graduated high school, of course. Not a bad gig, being drafted in the NHL before you even had your high school diploma.

Ryder spoke first, and decided to talk to the team about expectations, and always striving for more. "When we got together last year, we were a group of guys from all over. Canada, the United States, Russia, Sweden, Czech Republic. Some of us were drafted by the Generals, others came here via trade, and a few in free agency. For most of us, though, it was the expansion draft, after we'd been left unprotected by our former teams." That was the route Ryder took, having previously played for the New York Rangers. "Nobody knew what to expect from us, and we didn't know what to expect from ourselves. After all, we'd never played together before, yet we were somehow supposed to form a team. And we did.

"We lost our first game in spectacular fashion, but picked up a win in the next one, and soon more wins followed. And somewhere along the way, we formed our identity. We became a team. Even more than that, we became like a family." Maybe it sounded cheesy or cliched, but Ryder really did view these guys as an extension of his family. "We were there for each other through good and bad, and personal challenges." He looked at Trevor as he said it. "We may not be the most talented team, or the most experienced, but we stick together and give it our all, every day. I know we surprised a lot of people last season, and exceeded their expectations, but I think I can speak for most of us, if not all of us in this room, when I say we came up short, because our last game was a loss. We didn't take home the ultimate prize. Well, I don't know about you, but that jawed at me all summer, and I'm hungry. I want that prize. So let's get ready to play hockey!"

***

"Ryder, Alex and Colton just got done addressing the team, and they're about to take the ice for their first drills," Char announced to Jessica. "Ryder's in the first group, along with the new draft pick. The one from New Hampshire that hasn't even finished high school, if you can believe that."

"Okay..." Jessica said. "Is there some reason why you're giving me a play by play of the first day of training camp?" Char had invited her to lunch, presumably to get a recap of Jessica's date with Ryder, and so far she'd spent most of the time on her phone, following the Generals' twitter feed, and providing Jessica with a running commentary.

"Sorry. Force of habit. I do work for the team." Char set her phone down. "That and I figured you might be interested in knowing what Ryder is up to today."

"Why would I be interested?" Jessica kept her tone nonchalant.

Char shrugged. "Oh, I don't know. You haven't killed me yet, or even threatened to again, so I'm guessing your date with Ryder must have gone well." The self-satisfied smile returned to her face. "I did good, didn't I?"

Jessica sipped diet soda through a straw and rolled her eyes. "Don't break your arm patting yourself on the back," she said. "But yes, it went fine. The food and the music were good. We had a nice time."

"Yep. Exactly as I expected," Char said, making an exaggerated motion of patting her shoulder. "I did real good. So, when are you seeing him again?"

She was so pleased with herself, Jessica almost hated to burst her bubble. Almost, but not quite. "My guess would be never."

"What?" Char's eyes widened in apparent horror. "You just said things went well."

Jessica nodded. "They did, yes. And I told Ryder he can call me at the station if he's interested in seeing me again. I don't expect to hear from him, though. Once the hockey season starts, he's going to forget all about me. He probably already has."

"You don't know that." Char sighed. "Why do you say things like that?"

"Because I am naturally cynical about relationships." There. She'd said it. Jessica didn't like it, but it was a fact. But in her defense, everyone was a product of their experiences and their surroundings. And hers told her that this wouldn't be something that worked out. It couldn't be. "And because I've already spent enough time with Ryder to know what he wants most out of life," she said. "It's not a relationship. It's not a family. It's a silver trophy with a bowl on the top."

***

The first day of training camp consisted only of drills, focusing on skating, puck battles, and positional assignments. They'd get into scrimmage situations on day two, before taking the ice for the intrasquad Maroon versus Silver game on day three. After that, the team would head back to San Antonio for its first preseason game. Most of the younger prospects would probably not be with the team beyond that game, instead rejoining their junior leagues. But at least they'd get a taste of an NHL camp, and hopefully want a lot more.

Ryder got to spend the afternoon session working with the newest addition, and it was easy to see why Ryan Howton-Canfield had impressed the team's scouts enough to be drafted as a seventeen-year-old who hadn't even finished high school. The kid's moves were raw, and he needed to gain strength on the puck. He was a prospect, in every sense of the word, and wouldn't be ready for the pro leagues for several years, but he skated well and had a powerful shot. It wasn't hard to imagine him eventually wearing a Generals uniform, especially since the team's management had preached from the beginning a desire to develop talent from within.

"Mr. Carrigan?" Ryan approached him after

they'd wrapped up their drills session.

"My name is Ryder. We're teammates now."
Even if the kid was twelve years younger.

"Yeah, for a couple more days, 'til I get sent
back home." Ryan brushed his damp, sandy blond hair
away from his youthful face.

To finish high school. Not a bad gig. 'How'd
you spend your summer vacation?' 'Oh, I participated
in my first NHL training camp.' Could anyone top that?
Ryder doubted it. "Hey, if you keep on working hard,
you'll be in San Antonio in no time. Or at least here in
El Paso for starters."

"I'm cool with that," the kid said. "My mom
went to law school not far from here, in Grande Valley.
Anyway, I just wanted to say how much I enjoyed
practicing with you today. I know you don't remember,
but I met you nine years ago when you played for the
Hartford Wolfpack. You signed my jersey."

Ryder didn't remember. He'd spent two years in
Hartford before being called up to the Rangers, and met
plenty of kids during that time, and signed plenty of
ball caps, pucks and jerseys. He must've made an
impression on this one. "Wow. Small world."

"For sure. Anyway, I'd just started playing
hockey at the time, and you were my favorite player. So
being here, practicing with you, this is a dream."

"Thanks, Ryan. You've earned this, though.
You've got real talent," Ryder said. "Who knows?
Maybe we'll play on a line together in a few years." It
wasn't entirely impossible. At thirty, Ryder still had
some good years left in his career, and he hoped to
finish it with the Generals.

"Man, that would be awesome." The kid

grinned. "No matter what, this will be the best three days of my life," he said. "And I hope you guys win the Cup this year."

"Me, too," Ryder said. "We're going after it." Eyes on the prize. There was no room for distractions. Too bad he couldn't stop thinking about Jessica Rowan and when he might see her again. *Damn it, Ryder. Get a grip. Get your priorities right.*

MICHELE SHRIVER

CHAPTER SEVEN

It took a few days, but Ryder did call, and Jessica wasn't sure how to handle it when he did. She'd wanted to hear from him again, certainly. But she hadn't expected it. Then suddenly there he was, calling her at the news station, exactly as she'd told him he could do.

"How was El Paso?" she asked, after struggling to know what to say.

"Hot." Ryder laughed. "But it's hot here, too. We had a good camp, though. Excited about some of the new kids coming in, even if they're heading back to juniors soon. We have a good future," he said, and it was impossible to miss the enthusiasm in Ryder's voice.

"That's good," Jessica said.

"Yeah. So how are you?" he asked.

"I'm okay. Busy. There was a sexual assault on the university campus."

"Ouch," Ryder said. "I'm sorry."

"Reporting violent crimes is never a fun part of my job," Jessica said. "Especially crimes against women."

"I'm sure. So what's your schedule like?" he asked. "I mean, you get to eat dinner, right?"

"Yes," Jessica said, chuckling a little. What was he getting at? It was hard to tell. "I do the news at six." She glanced at her watch. It was close to four, meaning rush time was about to start. That last frantic period before they went live on the air. "It goes until six thirty, but I'm sure you knew that. After that, I'm sort of free for a couple of hours, before it's time to do the race all over again to be ready for ten o'clock." It was a hectic pace, for sure, but one Jessica loved, even if she did wonder how it would all work if she ever got married and had a family. Assuming anyone would ever want to put up with this schedule.

"So do you leave? After the six o'clock, I mean?"

"I can..." Jessica hedged. "Usually, I stay. I like to use the time to prep for the late newscast." That and she had no life, but she was less inclined to admit that. "You never know what might happen." Was she making excuses now?

"Sure, right," Ryder said. "But it sounds like you do get a break for dinner, even if you don't want to leave the station. Is that right?"

"Something like that." Insisting otherwise would only be lying.

"Perfect," Ryder said. "Then I'll bring dinner by for the two of us, after the early the newscast. Does that sound like a plan?"

Any protest that Jessica might have faded quickly. Who could resist a handsome hockey player bringing them dinner, even if the relationship didn't ultimately go anywhere? "Sure, yes. I look forward to it."

"Then I'll see you soon," Ryder said, before

hanging up.

Jessica set down the phone and buried herself in her work for next hour and a half. If Ryder showed up, great. If not, she wouldn't be shocked and she wouldn't dwell on it. She'd grab something from the cafeteria and get ready for the late news. It was what she did, day in and day out. And most of the time, Jessica still loved it, even if she did want more.

The alleged sexual assault at the university captivated the start of the news, along with a robbery on the east side. Combine that with Generals training camp, anticipation of the Spurs season, the upcoming university football game and the possibility of thunderstorms, and it made for a busy newscast with a lot to report.

"And fade. We're off the air in five. Four. Three. Two. One, and clear," the news director announced. "Good job."

Jessica breathed a sigh of relief. Even after doing this for six years, and knowing the routine like the back of her hand, she still experienced both the nerves of going live on the air, followed by the rush of adrenaline as the newscast shifted from the "headline" news to the weather and sports, and finally the sense of accomplishment as it all ended. At least until they did it all over again at ten o'clock.

"Nice job, Neil," Jessica said to her co-anchor. She unclipped the microphone from her shirt and pushed back her chair.

"You, too," he said. "Are you heading out for a bit now?"

She shook her head at the usual question, never knowing quite what to make of it. Neil was recently divorced. Was he simply being friendly, or interested in more? Either way, Jessica didn't want to jeopardize a good working relationship. "Not tonight. I have a friend coming by with dinner," she said. "I'll see you back here for the next race." Hopefully that wasn't too abrupt.

"Jess?" The station manager approached her as she left the set. "You do have a guest. He's waiting in conference room B," she said, then added with a wink, "And he's cute."

Jessica laughed at the same time she rolled her eyes. "Yes, I know he is. Thanks, Missy."

***

Ryder got to the news station just as Jessica and her co-anchor were about to go live for the early newscast, and was allowed to watch from the control room. Two things had immediately struck him: The newsroom was smaller than it appeared on TV, and Jess was a total professional. The skill and apparent ease with which she and her co-anchor moved between news segments impressed Ryder, especially since it seemed as if the news director was constantly barking orders. Then again, he could relate to that, because Coach Moreau never shut up, either.

As the broadcast neared its conclusion, Ryder was told he could wait in the conference room, and he used the time to set up their dinner, which he'd picked up from the deli a block over from the station. It wasn't anything fancy, but Ryder hoped Jess would appreciate the gesture.

The door pushed open. "Ryder? Missy said you

were in here. Hi."

"Hi." She looked different than she had the day they'd gone to the jazz festival, with her hair styled with soft waves, and more makeup, which Ryder figured was for television. Either way, she was beautiful. "Great job."

"Oh, you saw some of it?" Jessica asked.

"All of it." Ryder smiled. "I got here right before you went live." He'd done it on purpose, hoping he'd be allowed to watch. "You weren't kidding about a busy news day."

"It's crazy. Sometimes Neil and I joke that there's something in the city water supply, or people took their stupid pills." She shook her said. "But it's good for our ratings, at least. I'm sure you've heard the expression, 'If it bleeds, it leads.' Today was one of those days when we weren't even sure which blood to lead with," Jessica said dryly. "We may change it up for ten, since we have multiple options."

"That's rough," Ryder said, understanding more about the high-pressure job she worked in.

Jessica shrugged. "Unfortunately, I'm pretty used to it." Her eyes scanned the table. "I see you made good on your promise to bring dinner. This looks great. Is it from JP's around the corner?"

"Yep. I hope that's okay."

"Better than okay. It's one of my favorite places." She pulled out a chair and sat down. "If you by chance brought a turkey and provolone on a Ciabatta, with pesto mayo, I might love you forever."

It was clearly a joke, and Ryder was happy to play along. "In that case, we better get married," he quipped, pointing at one of the wrapped sandwiches. "That one's the turkey. I thought it sounded good, too."

"Oh, did you have your heart set on it?" Jessica frowned. "Because I can have something else..."

It was gracious to make the offer, especially when Ryder sensed Jessica didn't want to. No way would he take her up on it and deny her her favorite sandwich "No, please. That one's yours. I've fine with the ham and Swiss." He sat down and unwrapped the sandwich. "I can always come back, now that I know the place."

"And hopefully provide me with delivery," Jessica said.

"Well, I suppose. We are engaged, after all." Ryder hoped the joke hadn't grown stale, and fortunately Jess laughed.

"Now you know that the way to my heart is apparently through my stomach." She took a bite of her sandwich and washed it down with a swallow of soda. "Did you by chance bring the double fudge brownies for dessert?"

"I did," Ryder confirmed. It appeared he'd done quite well with his food selections.

"Yep. Then it's love." Jessica grinned as she opened a bag of the kettle chips. "Are you staying for the late newscast, too?"

He shook his head. "No, we have a game tomorrow, so I shouldn't be out too late, and I know you have work to do. I'm hoping you'll show me around a little after we eat, though. If you have time before you prepare for the ten o'clock."

"I do," Jessica said. "And I'm sure our sports reporter would love to meet you."

***

They ate and talked and laughed, and as Jessica polished off one of JP's famous fudge brownies, she wasn't quite ready for their date, if that's what it was, to end, and to have to go back to the set.

"How much time do you have?" Ryder asked, as if sensing her reluctance.

Jessica glanced at her watch. "Twenty minutes, tops, on a day like today." If it were a quiet news day, she might take more, but now she wouldn't risk it, no matter how attractive the company might be.

"I'll go, then," Ryder said, pushing back his chair. "I don't want to leave you rushed."

"I appreciate that, but at least let me introduce you to Brian, our sports guy."

"Sure, I'd like that."

Ryder helped her clean up the trash, and even let her have the last of the brownies to save for later, which Jessica gladly accepted. By the time she finished the late news, she'd be ready for a chocolate fix.

They left the conference room, and she found her colleague at work at his computer. "Brian? I have a friend I thought you'd want to meet."

The sports reporter turned away from his computer monitor and his eyes widened. "You're... Ryder Carrigan. From the Generals."

"I am." Ryder laughed and extended his hand.

"Brian Sparks. I cover sports here, and I'm a fan. I wish they'd send me out to some of your games, but there's only so much manpower and budget."

Ryder nodded. "So I guess we need to win a playoff series for you guys to take us seriously."

Jessica was momentarily alarmed. Was Ryder

offended that her station didn't expend more resources on covering his team? No. He seemed to be smiling. That was a good thing.

He made small talk with Brian for a few minutes before saying, "I should probably go, and let both of you get back to work."

Jessica walked him to the door. "Thanks again for bringing dinner. I appreciate it."

"I'm happy to do it. I wanted to see you again." Ryder rested his hand against the doorframe. "You're off tomorrow, right? Since it's the weekend?"

Jessica nodded. "Yes. Our weekend crew will be here." She'd welcome the break after such a busy week. "Why? Don't you have a game tomorrow?"

He nodded. "Yep. Against Colorado. I'm hoping you'll come watch us." He smiled. "I mean, I've seen what you do now. It's only fair for you to see what I do, what a day on the job is like for me."

CHAPTER EIGHT

Jessica found herself sitting in the eighth row, center ice, in a group that included Kristie Gray, wife of Alex, Angie Rollins, wife of Seth, Maya Dominguez, fiancée of team captain, Colton Tremblay, and an attractive redhead named Kendall Myers, whom Jessica learned dated the Generals' goaltender, Becker Lawson. Was this her official indoctrination into the WAGs club? She wasn't sure she was ready for that, not after only two dates. Yet here she was.

"Is Dani going to be here?" she asked. Not that the other women didn't all seem friendly enough, but she already had some prior acquaintance with Dani. The others, she'd met less than an hour ago.

Kristie shook her head. "I doubt it, since Trevor's not in the lineup tonight," she said. "Preseason, so they're evaluating different players. It'll be a mix of veterans and rookies."

"Oh, right." Jessica nodded. Ryder had mentioned something about that. Without the full team of veterans, he would be playing on the top line, alongside Colton, something she knew he looked forward to. "What about the new kid?" she asked. "The one they just drafted, who's still in high school."

"Back in history class, probably," Maya remarked. "He was sent home when the team left El Paso. Talented kid, but not ready for the big leagues."

"Oh." So much for trying to sound as if she knew what she was talking about. "Sorry. I'm pretty new to this."

Kendall gave her a sympathetic smile. "That's okay. So am I. Though I suppose I'm maybe at a slight advantage since my son plays hockey and is a huge fan of the team."

"We were all new to this at one time," Kristie said. "Heck, I didn't know the difference between a face off and a tip off when I first met Alex." She laughed. "Now I'm obsessed with hockey, to the extent that I can quote fancy stats like Corsi and Fenwick."

Angie rolled her eyes. "Yeah, Kris is our resident hockey geek. That stuff goes straight over my head. Anyway, you don't have to be a statistics nerd to enjoy the game. A basic, working knowledge is fine. You know, like try to put the puck in the other team's net, and keep it out of your own."

"I can handle that much," Jessica said.

"Great," Maya said. "Then welcome to the club."

So Jessica had been right. It was a club. "Thanks, I guess, but I'm not sure I'll be back for more games," she said. "I work most nights, and besides, Ryder and I aren't actually a couple."

"Really, now?" Angie laughed. "You could've

fooled me. I mean, you're here, aren't you?"

"Yes, but..."

"But nothing," Maya interrupted. "Look, we all know Ryder. He's Mr. Serious. Always so focused that the guys on the team, especially Noah, insist he doesn't even know to kick back and relax. I don't even think he had a date last year. He was probably studying film after every single loss. So for him to invite you here, to watch him play? That's a very big deal."

"She's right," Kristie said. "We all expect to see you again at future games."

"Oh," Jessica said. Apparently it was her new word of the night, proving that news reporters weren't always eloquent. She settled back into her seat, unsure what else to say. "Go Generals."

***

The energy inside the building was palpable, especially for a preseason game, and as soon as Ryder took the ice with the rest of the guys for warm-ups, he could tell they were in for a special season. Their fans were ready for hockey again. It seemed that the Generals' surprise appearance in the playoffs in their inaugural season, followed by the sting of the round loss, had whet their appetites for more. Ryder might want the Stanley Cup so badly he could practically taste it, but if the intensity of the crowd was any indication, they wanted it, too.

With a game day roster that included some Generals veterans, along with quite a few prospects, the line pairings were dramatically different from those at the end of the season. The absence of Nikolai Brantov meant Ryder got a chance to skate on Colton's left wing, a spot he'd fully intended to occupy the season before. Instead, Ryder was beaten out by the young Russian rookie, who claimed the spot on the top line straight out of training camp the year before and never surrendered it. Although disappointed, Ryder quickly formed a good chemistry skating on the second line with Casey and young Swede Cullen Jacobus. They'd had a lot of success, and Ryder expected to open the season with Casey and Cullen as his linemates once again.

Tonight, though, he got to skate with Colton on a line that included one of their talented prospects, Maks Klein, and they combined for an early goal against the Arizona Coyotes. Ryder scored off of a brilliant pass from Colton, with Maks tallying the secondary assist. As soon as the goal went in, Ryder raised his fist in the air, and as he skated toward the team bench for the customary fist bump with his teammates, he scanned the area a few rows behind the bench for Jessica. He spotted her right away, sitting next to Alex's wife, and she smiled as their eyes locked. Yes, hockey was back, and although Ryder wasn't accustomed to having anyone in the stands cheering him on, he quickly decided he liked it.

After the first goal, the rout was on, and Ryder notched two goals and an assist as San Antonio went soared to a decisive 4-1 victory against Arizona. It was only preseason, so there was no award of the toy gun holster to the best player, which was standard practice after regular season games. If they awarded it for preseason games, Ryder was fairly confident he would have won it. He still got plenty of fist bumps and back slaps from the rest of the guys, but Ryder didn't relish it in it. It was one game, and it didn't even count in the standings. They had a long season ahead and a lot of work to do.

A few of the guys were planning to go to a club after the game, and a few others were headed out to meet their significant others. Ryder wondered if Jessica had stayed to see him after the game, or already left to go home. He got his answer a few minutes later, as he left the arena with Alex and Colton. There, with Kristie and Maya, stood Jessica.

"Hey," he said, as he approached.

"Hi." Her eyes scanned up and down his body, and she smiled. "I guess it's true. You do always wear a suit to games."

"Yeah," he said. "Team rule."

"It's a good one. You like nice in suits."

"Thank you," Ryder said. She looked nice, too, wearing jeans that perfectly hugged her hips and a blue shirt with a plunging neckline that game just enough of a view of her cleavage to want to see more. He wanted to take her in his arms and kiss her. "Did you enjoy the game?"

She nodded. "I did. A lot."

"Great. You'll have to come to more oof them, at least on the weekends." Ryder shifted his bag to the other shoulder. "So what are you doing now?" he asked. "Do you want to go grab a late dinner or drink or something?"

A flicker of hesitation passed Jessica's eyes, as if she wanted to say yes, but ultimately she shook her head. "I'm going to have to pass. Not sure I'd be good company tonight, as tired as I am. It was a long week."

Having observed her during the live newscast the night before, Ryder understood, even if he was disappointed. "Some other time, then," he said. "I'll let you get your beauty sleep. Not that you need it. You're plenty beautiful already."

"And you're a smooth talker." The night sky outside the arena was dark, so Ryder couldn't tell if she blushed, but it wouldn't surprise him. "I'm free tomorrow, if you are."

"I am, yes." It was the team's day off, before departing on Monday for Arizona to play a rematch with the Coyotes, this time on their home ice. "Would you like to come over in the afternoon?" he asked. "I can grill some burgers, and we can take a swim."

"That sounds good. I'd enjoy that," Jessica said. "What time?"

"I don't know. Maybe three?"

She nodded. "Sure. That sounds good."

"Perfect." Ryder gave her his address. "I'll see you then."

"I'm looking forward to it," she said.

"Me too." Ryder started to walk in the direction of his car, then changed his mind and turned around.

"Did you forget something?" Jessica asked.

"Yes. I forgot to do this." Ryder lowered his head and brushed his lips softly across hers. They tatsed of cherry, probably the lip gloss she wore, and he wanted to taste more, but he pulled away. "Now I'm looking forward to tomorrow even more."

CHAPTER NINE

Jessica pulled into the driveway of a stunning home in the Elm Creek area and did a double-take. Yes, this was the address Ryder had given her. She was in the right place. Wow. She knew the NHL paid well, even if the salaries paled in comparison to the NFL or NBA, so maybe she shouldn't be shocked. Still, it was, quite simply, the most beautiful house she'd ever seen.

Ryder had told her to come around to the back when she got there, so Jessica did, finding him standing at an outdoor grill, wearing only a pair of board shorts in the design of the Canadian flag. *Nothing like a sexy guy with a Maple Leaf on his butt.* He must have heard her approach, or sensed her presence, because he turned around, revealing the same Maple Leaf pattern on the front of his shorts. The image sent Jessica's mind straight into the nearest gutter, and not simply because of his well-toned abs. Those didn't hurt the view any, though.

"Hi," he greeted her. "I guess you found me."

"I did, yes. Only got lost once," Jessica said. "Nice

house." Okay, that was a huge understatement. She looked around the expansive back yard, which featured a cobblestone patio with an outdoor kitchen. Beyond that was a pool with an adjoining hot tub, and the entire area was surrounded by tall trees and lush greenery. If there was another house nearby, Jessica couldn't see one. "It's like you have your own private greenbelt back here."

"Yeah, that's what I love about this place," Ryder said. "I just started the grill, and it's charcoal, so it will take a while to heat up."

"That's okay," Jessica said. "It's still early."

"That's what I figured. We can have a drink, maybe take a swim."

Jessica looked at the pool again. It was definitely enticing, especially on a warm day, and she'd come prepared. "That sounds like a good idea."

"Great. I'll go grab us some drinks from inside. Feel free to jump in the pool."

"I might do that." Jessica watched him head into the house, then moved to set her bag down on the chaise lounge by the pool. She pulled off the tank top and shorts she wore over her bikini and walked over to the edge of the pool, dipping one toe in. Not bad. Since the temperature seemed pleasant, she lowered her whole body into the pool. Okay. Still not bad. She went underwater, wetting her hair, and wiped it out of her face as she resurfaced. Still no sign of Ryder, so Jessica swam the length of the pool, then turned and swam back. As she returned back where she'd started, she noticed Ryder standing there watching. He held a bottle of wine in one hand, and two glasses in the other.

"How's the water?" he asked.

"Perfect. Are you coming in?"

"Maybe in a little bit." He held up the bottle. "Got some wine if you want some."

"I do," Jessica said. "Let me swim another lap or two, and I'll be right out."

***

Ryder had planned on getting in the pool, too, but rethought the strategy, instead being content to watch Jessica swim. His process of opening a bottle of wine had taken far longer than necessary, simply because he enjoyed the view so much from the kitchen window as she stripped down to her bikini. If she wasn't perfect, she was pretty darn close, with a tight, firm ass and ample breasts and flat stomach. He didn't mean to stare, but it was pretty hard not to.

He focused on pouring wine, and not spilling it, and fortunately had completed that task before Jessica emerged from the pool, or he probably would have spilled it for sure. Ryder sucked in his breath as she walked toward him, a soaking wet vision in a minimal bikini. Ryder tried to get his libido under control He wasn't Casey. He could behave himself. They'd have a drink, he'd fix dinner. They'd eat and talk. Then perhaps later, if Jessica was interested, things might progress further. *Please, be interested.*

"Wine?" he asked, holding out a glass.

"Yeah, just a minute. Do you have a towel?" She rubbed her hands over her arms. "It's kind of chilly when you get out of the water."

Sure enough, her nipples were erect under her bikini top, and even though Ryder was sure it was because of the chill she'd mentioned, rather than any sexual desire, the effect on him was more of the latter. "Of course, sorry. I should've had some out." He walked over to the bench storage unit, and flipped up the lid, grabbing a towel. He unfolded it and held it out for her, expecting her to simply take it from him. Instead, Jessica allowed him to wrap it around her and envelope her in his arms, something he didn't mind at all. "Better?" Ryder asked. "Are you warmer now?"

"Yes."

"Good." They stood in each other's arms for a moment, water dripping down her, their faces inches apart.

"Ryder?"

"Yeah?"

"Are you going to kiss me now?" Jessica's lips twitched. "I mean, I'm pretty sure you want to and you're just trying to be a gentleman and all—"

He didn't allow her finish the sentence, instead silencing her with a hungry kiss. How well she knew him after only a short time. With her permission, though, Ryder was more than happy to escalate things. He'd gotten a small taste of her the night before, and now he definitely wanted more.

So, apparently, did Jessica, as she responded immediately to the kiss, even nibbling on Ryder's bottom lip. He didn't know what it was about a nibble on the lip, but it had always turned him on. The effect was even greater with Jessica doing the nibbling, and Ryder felt the blood rushing to his lower region and his cock stiffen.

The towel dropped, and Ryder pushed himself against her, caressing Jessica's back before cupping her buttocks in his hands. His tongue still dancing with hers, Ryder used his hands to lift her butt cheeks and pulled her closer to him, grinding her crotch into his erection. He was hard for her, and he wanted her to know it.

"Oh, God, Ryder." Her words came out in a breathless pant as her lips came free of his and she looked up at him, her brown eyes heavy with arousal.

"We should probably go inside," he suggested.

"No, here," Jessica said. "I want you right here."

The very suggestion made Ryder's heart race. There was nothing he wanted more than to take her, right then and there, exactly as she'd requested. His patio was certainly private enough, so that wasn't an issue, but he wasn't prepared. He'd thought of everything else, but not protection. *Damn it*. He silently cursed himself. "I... I don't have anything out here."

"I do," Jessica said. "In my bag. Just a minute."

She'd come prepared with condoms in her bag, is that what she was saying? Ryder's mind raced, wondering if she always carried them with her, or if she'd made a point of packing them today, in the expectation—hope?—that something like this might happen. He much preferred the latter to the former, but at the moment didn't really care. He wanted her, she wanted him, and she held a condom in her hand. What else mattered?

He led her to the chaise lounge, pulling her down into his lap. Jessica ripped open the condom packet, and Ryder tugged at the Velcro fly of his shorts, freeing his cock. As he did, he noticed Jessica's lips curl in amusement.

"Something funny?"

"No." She shook her head. "It's just as soon as I got here earlier, and saw the location of that maple leaf on your shorts, my mind started thinking dirty things. And now here you are, and your erection is poking through that maple leaf, and..."

"It's funny?" That wasn't the effect he'd been going for.

"No. It's sexy, hot. Really hot." Jessica reached out and stroked him with her hands before sheathing him with the condom, then moved on top of him. With her hand, she pushed the skimpy fabric of her bikini bottom to the side, allowing for entry and impaled herself on him.

Ryder held her hips and pushed upward, entering her all the way. God, yes, she felt good. Firm and tight around his shaft. "You okay, baby?"

"Perfect. You Canadian boys are sure big and hard, but that's exactly the way I like it," she said, as she began to move on top of him.

***

Jessica struggled to catch her breath. She didn't know what came over her. She didn't talk like that, and she wasn't usually quite so aggressive, either. Then again, she was a firm believer in seizing opportunities when they presented themselves, and this one definitely had. Hello! Sexy athlete. Gorgeous, inviting pool. Private back yard, with no chance anyone could see or hear them. It was the ideal set-up for spontaneous sex and mind-blowing orgasms, right?

"My God. Wow." Ryder seemed to be having difficulty recovering, too.

"My sentiments exactly." Since she seemed to have control of her breathing again, Jessica shifted off of him and adjusted her bathing suit.

"I... the grill. I should probably check the grill." Ryder pulled the condom off and set it on the ground, then tucked himself back inside his shorts. "The coals are probably plenty hot by now."

Jessica stifled a chuckle. The coals weren't the only thing that had gotten hot. "I would imagine so. Is there anything I can do to help?"

He shook his head. "No, I got this. Relax. Drink your wine."

"Okay, if you're sure." She'd almost forgotten the wine, but there it sat, undisturbed on the table a few feet away. As Ryder went into the house, presumably to get the food, Jessica picked up a glass and took a drink, settling onto the chaise lounge. He was back a few minutes later, carrying a tray of food. Much to her disappointment, Jessica noticed he'd put a T shirt on, too.

"I've got a salad, and my famous pizza burgers," Ryder said.

"Famous, huh?"

He shrugged. "Well, maybe not famous, but I like to think they're good," he said. "It's the recipe I put in the charity cookbook."

"Oh, yeah. Char told me about the project. It's coming out this fall, right?"

"Yes." Ryder set the tray down on the table, then carried the plate with the burgers on it to the grill. "Hopefully people enjoy it. It's a good collection of our favorite recipes."

"I know Char's excited."

Ryder put the burgers on the grill, then walked back toward her. "How's the wine?'

"Very good, thank you." So they weren't going to talk about what happened, rather just move on to dinner and small talk. Good. That suited Jessica fine. She didn't feel the need to dissect or analyze anything. They were two attractive, single, consenting adults acting on a basic human desire. What needed to be discussed?

Apparently, Ryder felt the same way. They ate the salad while they chatted about the game, her work, the wine, and his house, with Ryder promising her a grand tour later. When the burgers were ready, he brought hers to her on a plate and they sat there on the patio furniture eating while they talked and laughed.

She could see why the recipe was a favorite of his, because she liked it, too. It obviously wasn't low fat, with pepperoni, black olives and pizza sauce stuffed inside a burger and topped with mozzarella, but it tasted great. At the moment, that was all Jessica cared about.

After they'd eaten, Jessica helped Ryder carry the dishes into the house. She offered to load the dishwasher, but he brushed her off, and instead they went back outside, and lay together on the chaise lounge while they sipped another glass of wine.

"Are you up for a moonlight swim?" Ryder asked as the sun began to set beyond the horizon.

"Sure." Jessica wasn't ready for the evening to end.

"Great." Ryder got up, discarded his T-shirt and jumped in the pool, while Jessica hesitated. "Aren't you coming in?" he asked.

"I am, yeah." She was more interested in a little more naughty fun than the swim, though. "But I've got too much clothing on. And so do you."

***

Ryder stood in the shallow end of the pool, staring as Jessica removed her bikini bottoms, followed by the top, until she stood there, completely nude. He was pretty sure his jaw dropped open. After all, even though he'd made love to her, he'd yet to see her naked before now. Man, she was incredible. Her breasts, her ass, her slender, narrow waist. All of it. Water be damned, Ryder's cock responded.

"Too many clothes, huh? Well, let's see about that." He untied his shorts and yanked open the fly before stepping out of them, then tossed them out of the pool. "Is this better?" Ryder asked, as he stood, half underwater, with the tip of his erect penis sticking out above the water.

Jessica stared at it as she broke out in a grin. "That's much more like it, yeah, big guy. Just a minute. I think we still need something." She turned around, giving him a perfect view of her butt as she fished around in her bag, then tossed something into the pool.

It took Ryder only a second to realize what it was, and he thanked the heavens above for Jessica's sense of preparation as he lunged for the condom packet. He grabbed it in his hand and moved to the steps of the shallow end and far enough out of the water to cover himself. He turned to find Jessica perched on the side of the pool, legs spread, and her hand between them as she touched herself.

Ryder's breath caught in his throat. "Are you ready, or do you need longer?" *Because I don't mind watching.*

"I'm ready," she answered, moving her hand out of

the way and spreading her legs wider.

If there was a sight more inviting Ryder didn't know what it was. "Have I told you lately you're incredible?" He asked, moving in between her legs, ready to enter her.

"Maybe. If not, you can tell me by showing me."

No way was he passing on that request.

***

They finally did get the swim in, better late than never, but it didn't last long as a chill settled into the air once the sun was fully down. It was hard to complain, though. It was the end of September. Plenty of people in other places had to drain their pools by now and cover them for the season. In Texas, it was pool season almost year round.

Still, Jessica was cold as she rushed into Ryder's house with a towel wrapped around her. Yikes! She should have thought of this and packed something else to wear, but no... she'd brought condoms, but not a change of clothes. The former had sure come in handy, but she longed for the latter, too. "Brr." She let out an involuntary shiver. It was okay. Ryder would give her a robe and they'd cuddle by the fireplace, or else he'd take her to his bed and hold her in his arms until she warmed up. Either was fine.

"Yeah, it got cool in a hurry," he said. "Let me grab you a T-shirt and a pair of sweat pants to put on. You can give them back to me later."

"What?" Jessica's brain struggled to catch up. Was he kicking her out? Surely not...

"You know, so you're not cold driving home."

Surely yes. What the hell? "Oh. Right." Jessica couldn't disguise her clipped tone. "Thanks. That's very generous." Neither could she disguise the sarcasm.

"Wait, what?" Ryder had the decency to look confused. "Oh, shit." He put his palm to his forehead. "You were expecting to stay, weren't you?"

Well, duh, asshole! We did just have sex twice... "No, it's okay. Never mind."

"Are you sure? I mean, that'd be nice and all, but I have to be at the rink really tomorrow for a skate, then we're flying to Phoenix..."

Excuses, excuses. They weren't original or creative ones, though. It was always the team. Yes, she'd made a huge mistake tonight. No doubt about that. Jessica wasn't inclined to compound it. No. She only wanted to get away with what little was left of her dignity. "Fine. Just give me the damn sweatpants, Ryder, and I'll get out of your way."

MICHELE SHRIVER

CHAPTER TEN

Ryder could usually tell when he'd messed up, and this was no exception. Jessica's icy tone told him everything he needed to hear, and then some. He'd screwed up in a very big way. "Okay, I can see that you're mad—"

"Brilliant deduction, Sherlock. Now can I have those pants, please?"

"Fine, okay." He rushed to his bedroom, and returned a minute later with a pair of drawstring sweats and a T-shirt. "Here, put these on, and let's talk about this."

"Talk?" Jessica laughed, but there was no humor in it. "First, you demand that I leave, and now you want to talk about?"

"What? I didn't demand that you leave. I said you shouldn't stay."

"Semantics, Ryder." Jessica yanked the pants on and cinched the waist, then pulled the T-shirt over her head. Even dressed in his baggy clothes, she was beautiful. Not that she'd want to hear that right now.

"I told you why. It's nothing personal," he tried to explain. "I just have to be up super early to get to the rink."

"Of course. You need your beauty sleep, and you don't want me interfering with it. I might distract you or something. We wouldn't want that." Ouch. She'd mastered the art of sarcasm, that's for sure. "Sweet dreams, Ryder, and good luck in Arizona."

"Thanks, I think." The words were nice, but he doubted the sincerity. He followed her to the door. "I'll call you when I get back in town."

Jessica had her hand on the doorknob, and turned around. "Why? So we can do this again? Don't bother." She pulled the door open and stormed out, leaving Ryder standing in the doorway, watching as her car pulled out of the driveway and disappeared down the street.

Son of a bitch. *Smooth, Ry. Real smooth.* He closed the door and went back in the house. He'd ruined it with Jess, and he still had a whole kitchen of dirty dishes to clean up. The afternoon may have started out promising, but it sure went to hell in a hurry. And Ryder had no one to blame for that but himself.

***

No. She wouldn't cry. She wouldn't. She might be hurt and humiliated, and feel like an idiot, but Jessica was determined not to cry. No. She'd just have to chalk this one up to experience. One more bad relationship. Except she wasn't even sure this one could even classify as a relationship. What had it lasted? Three dates? Okay, four if she counted the hockey game, but that was a stretch. *Yeah, good work, Jess.*

Instead of driving home, she headed to Char's house. One thing Jessica could always count on was her best friend being home alone on a Sunday night, and probably working. Char arguably had an even worse social life than Jessica, if such a thing were possible. Maybe they were even, in the most pathetic way possible.

Jessica rang the bell, and Char answered, wearing yoga pants, a tank top, and her glasses perched on her nose. Yep. Working. "What are you doing here? I thought you were with Ryder." Char frowned. "And why are you dressed like you just had a break up and you plan to spend the night on the couch eating cookie dough ice cream and watching *Bridget Jones' Diary*?"

Jessica couldn't help but laugh. "It wasn't intentional, but that's rather fitting," she said. "Can I come in?"

"Of course, silly." Char stepped out of the way to let her in. "I have no social life, and my door's always open to you."

"Thanks."

"You are going to tell me what's going on, though, right?"

Jessica nodded. "Yeah. You have wine, right?"

It was Char's turn to laugh. "Is the sky blue? Is Texas hot in the summer? Have a seat. I'll be right back."

Jessica made her way to Char's a living room, and took a seat on the couch, folding her legs Indian style. She noticed Char's laptop sitting on the coffee table, confirming her friend had, indeed, been working. Probably crunching numbers for the Generals' foundation or brainstorming more fundraising activities. Char was tireless in her dedication to the hockey club and charitable activities. Jessica could relate, because she shared a similar dedication to her own work. Maybe it was time to focus entirely on it and give up the idea of a relationship.

"Here you go." Char was back, handing Jessica a glass of white wine.

"Thanks." Jessica accepted it and took a drink, recognizing it as one of her favorite Chardonnays. "What a day."

"So what happened?" Char sat down beside her, propping her bare feet on the coffee table. "You didn't have a good time with Ryder?"

"Oh, I had a great time with Ryder," Jessica said. She eyed the clock on the wall. "Until about half an hour ago, that is." She exhaled. "His house is incredible, and his pizza burgers are really good, and he's funny, and sexy. Very sexy." Jessica took another drink. "I blew it, Char."

"Blew it how?"

"I don't know... maybe I was too playful, too aggressive, or assumed too much." The latter for sure. "We had sex. Twice. Once out by his pool, and once inside the pool. He has this gorgeous backyard and pool, all surrounded by huge, lush trees. It's totally private, and I just... got turned on, and so did he, and no one could see us, so why not?" Jessica closed her eyes for a second, recalling how he'd entered her as perched on the edge of the pool. No foreplay whatsoever, and she'd probably have a rash on her buttocks from rubbing on the concrete, but at the time, she hadn't cared. It felt so good, so primal, being naked under the stars as he thrust away inside her, until she finally exploded with such a mind blowing climax that she'd screamed, and loudly.

"It was naughty, and completely unlike me, but my God, it was hot, Char."

"It sounds like it." Char set her glass on a coaster on the table, and turned to face Jessica. "Which begs the question. Why are you here, and not still with Ryder, going for round three?"

"Oh, believe me, that's what I wanted, and expected. I figured we'd make it to his bed, and since we got the reckless desire out of the way, he'd make slow, beautiful love to me, then he'd hold me in his arms as I fell asleep." She rolled her eyes. "Well, I guess the joke's on me. Ryder wanted nothing to do with that. He has practice tomorrow, and then they fly to their next game, so he needs his rest, you know." Jessica practically spit the words out. "So once he got his rocks off, he was anxious to be rid of me. He did, at least, let me borrow these lovely clothes so I wasn't cold on the drive."

"What?" Char's eyes widened. "He kicked you out? On the street."

"Not kicked out, exactly. He just made it clear I wasn't welcome to stay."

"Semantics."

"Right!"

"He's an asshole," Char declared with a sigh. "I'm sorry, Jess. I feel responsible. I got you into this."

She shook her head. "It's not your fault. And I really don't think he's an asshole." Why was she defending him? "Just too focused on hockey and socially clueless."

"Maybe. I guess," Char said. "I suppose there might be one bright side?"

"What's that?"

"You don't have to do the walk of shame before dawn."

"Whatever." Jessica didn't find it much solace as she drained her glass. "Do you have more of this?"

"Do you even have to ask?" Chat took the empty glass from her. "Plenty more, but I'm not letting you drive home. You're sleeping in the guest room."

"Fine." Jessica smiled. "You're a good friend, Char. Even if you did set me up with Ryder."

***

So much for getting a good night's sleep. Ryder doubted whether he got any sleep at all. He was way too preoccupied with how badly he'd ruined things with Jessica, and as a result was in a lousy mood when he got to practice rink for the team's skate before leaving for Arizona. It wasn't lost on his teammates, either.

"Okay, what gives?" Casey wanted to know. "You're acting like something crawled up your ass and bit you."

"Shut up," Ryder muttered. "I'm just tired. I didn't get much sleep."

"Ooh, up too late with the sexy news anchor, eh?" Casey grinned. "It's about damn time, Carrigan. I was beginning to wonder if you had it in you."

"Bite me."

Casey laughed. "Okay, scratch that. You're in way too pissy of a mood to have gotten laid last night."

Ryder glared at him. "As a matter of fact, I did get

laid last night."

"Yeah? So what's the problem? It wasn't good?"

Ryder clenched his teeth. He liked Casey, and knew most of what he said was all in jest, but sometimes it got a little overdone and Ryder wanted to slap him. "Actually, it was great," he said. Maybe he could make Casey a little jealous, given his own attraction to Jessica. Then again, Casey already had a bevy of women. He didn't need any more.

"So what's the problem, then?"

"We had a little fight afterwards." If it even qualified as a fight. "She assumed she'd be spending the night, but that wasn't possible, because I had to be here first thing this morning." Now it sounded lame even to Ryder. Not just lame. Jack-assish.

"So you kicked her out?" Casey shook his head. "Fuck, man, you're even more clueless than I thought. You can entertain a woman in your bed overnight and still make it to practice on time." He laughed. "I'm proof of that. I do it all the time. Just takes a good alarm clock."

"Shut up," Ryder hissed. "Not all of us are man whores like you."

"Too bad. If you were, you might not be lamenting your lack of skills with the opposite sex right now."

"Ha. You're funny." *Or not at all.*

"Are you both done?" Colton skated up in front of them. "Because this is supposed to be a hockey practice, not a debate on who's worse with women," he said. "Though from what I heard, you both have some work to do. At least you're slightly better at hockey."

"I'm done, yes," Ryder said. "Conversation over. Let's practice, then go kick some Coyote ass." It was time to focus now. He'd have to find a way to fix things with Jessica when he got home. Whatever it took.

CHAPTER ELEVEN

Ryder tried to call Jessica late in the morning, and again in the afternoon. She assumed the calls were made before the team left for Arizona, and then again after they arrived. Not that it mattered, because Jessica ignored them both. He was probably calling to apologize and try to fix things, and while she would like the apology, Jessica was far less interested in fixing things with Ryder. She also didn't want to get sucked into any drama on a busy news day. Deep down, she knew that was the real reason for avoiding Ryder's calls. He had the ability to unsettle her and mess up her concentration and focus, and that scared Jessica, because it meant he'd gotten under her skin, and she already felt something for him. Damn it! The last thing she needed was to fall for a hockey player who cared about more about the Stanley Cup than any woman he'd ever date.

Instead, she focused on work, which was easy enough to do on a busy Monday for news. So busy, in fact, that she didn't even take a break for dinner between the six and ten o'clock shows, instead opting only grab a bag of pretzels from the vending machine, which she munched at her desk while she prepared.

The first ten minutes of a newscast that were always the most stressful, at least for anchors. After that, it transitioned to weather and sports, and they got to relax, at least a little, when they weren't on camera. After updates on the Spurs and UTSA's football team, and a profile on a local high school student who hoped to earn a college football scholarship, Brian gave an update on the Generals score. 3-0 Coyotes at the end of the second. Ouch.

"Tough break for the Generals," Brian said, once the broadcast was over and the cameras had cut away. "It's hard to tell much with no TV or radio coverage, but it sure sounds like they're having a rough game."

"Yeah," Jessica said. "It's only preseason, though. They'll get it together." Still, given Ryder's competitive spirit, he had to be pretty angry right now. Angry and disappointed.

"I hope so," the sportscaster said. "Thanks for introducing me to Ryder the other day. He seems like a nice guy."

Oh, yeah. He's a real prince. "I suppose so." She didn't feel much like defending him, but neither did Jessica want to bad mouth him. She only wanted this conversation to be over.

Brian nodded. "All right, see you later." He stood up and left the news desk, giving Jessica her wish.

Jessica pushed her chair back. She was ready for the day to be done and to get home to her own house and her own bed, having spent the night in Char's guest room after drinking too much wine.

"Hey, Jess?"

She turned to her co-anchor. "Yes, Neil?"

"I'm curious... that guy from the hockey team that was here the other day... Ryker?"

"Ryder." Obviously Neil wasn't a hockey fan.

"Ryder, right. Anyway, I'm just wondering, are you seeing him?"

Jessica hesitated. Why was Neil so curious about her relationship status with Ryder? She suspected she knew, and there was one way to ward off his questioning. Lie. Except she couldn't. "I went out with him a couple times, but it's nothing serious, and it's done now," she said. "Why?"

"I was hoping maybe you'd like to go out with me," Neil said. "You know, dinner or something, during our break between shows. "I'd like to get to know you better, Jess."

So there it was. Neil was interested. And Jessica had no idea how to let him down gently. Besides, maybe she needed to keep an open mind. Give him a chance. Get to know him. Who knows. She might find out they had a lot in common. Okay, probably not. But what was the harm in sharing one meal with him? "Sure," she said. "I'd like that. How about tomorrow, after the six o'clock?"

"Sounds good." Neil smiled. "It's a date."

***

The final horn sounded, and Ryder slammed his stick against the boards with so much force that he broke it. The team lost, and it wasn't just any loss. It was a completely humiliating one. Not quite as bad as the first regular season game in Generals history, but pretty darn close.

While the Coyotes players stayed on the ice after the game ended, enjoying the cheers of their home crowd after their 5-1 victory, Ryder and teammates hurried back to the visitor's locker room. Time for quick showers and a brief media session before boarding the charter plane back to San Antonio.

"Damn it!" Ryder yanked off his gloves and tossed him into his locker.

"Something wrong?" Noah Mann asked.

Was he serious? Probably not. Noah was seldom serious, and it drove Ryder crazy. "Yes. In case you didn't notice, we lost. 5-1. We were freaking humiliated out there."

Noah nodded. "Yeah, we lost. And it sucked. But it's only one game, and still preseason. It'll get better."

"Is everything a joke to you, Mann? Maybe you should try taking something serious for a change.

"What? Did you really just ask me that?" Noah shook his head, his damp, shaggy brown hair falling over his forehead. "No, everything isn't a joke to me. I would've thought you'd clued into that, after being teammates for a year. I give my all for this team. Blood, sweat, and even tears on a few occasions. Just because I like to goof around sometimes doesn't change that. Not that I'd expect you to get it, since you don't seem to know how to relax. Ever. Here's a bit of advice for you, Ry. Find some balance in your life, or you're gonna end up driving people away. If you haven't already done it."

Noah walked off in the direction of the shower, and Ryder sank onto the bench in front of his locker. Is that he was doing? Was he driving people away because he was too serious? He'd sure succeeded in hurting Jessica, and all because he'd prioritized a preseason hockey game over her. Even if he hadn't intended to, he knew it looked that way to her.

"Is something wrong, Ry?" Colton came over and sat beside him. "You've been wound tighter than a drum since practice this morning, and I couldn't help but notice how you just lit into Noah."

"I hate losing," Ryder said.

Colton nodded. "Fair enough. Show me a professional athlete who likes losing, and I'll show you someone who has no business being a professional athlete. But I think I've got a pretty good read on this team, and all the guys on it, and let me tell you, that's not Noah. That guy's as serious as you, me, anyone else, when it comes game time," Colton said, "and he feels the losses, too. Just because he likes to joke around doesn't mean he's not serious about the game."

Ryder exhaled sharply. "I know that. I do. And I'll apologize to Noah. I'm in a bad mood today, but I shouldn't take it out on him, or any of you guys."

"Yeah, we all noticed you're in a lousy mood," Colton said. "Some of the guys are making wagers as to why." He laughed. "That's not my thing, though, so I'll only say this. Whatever it is, figure it out. It's a long season, one that hasn't even really started yet. If we're going to reach our goals, we need everyone at their best."

"Understood," Ryder said. Now he had to figure out how to get there. He liked Jessica. He wanted to spend more time with her. He should be able to do that and still give his all to the game he loved. Plenty of other guys did it, so why was it so hard for him? Noah was right. Ryder's problem was balance, or lack thereof. There had to be a way to achieve it, though.

CHAPTER TWELVE

It wasn't a long flight back to San Antonio from Phoenix, but it nonetheless gave Ryder plenty of time to think. So did another sleepless night. Normally after a road game, with three days before the next game, morning skate would be optional. Not during the preseason, though, when the team was still evaluating players.

Ryder was happy to have practice. The loss still gnawed at him, and he was anxious to get back to work. He also had some repairs to make in his relationships with teammates, too, starting with Noah. He'd always prided himself on being a good teammate and a good leader, and worthy of wearing the 'A' on his sweater, but now, for the first time, Ryder questioned whether he deserved it. He'd been a first class jerk lately. First to Jessica, then to Noah.

He was early to the practice rink, but he wasn't the first one there. Noah was already in his gear and taking shots at an empty net. Ryder waved, and Noah skated over to him.

"Morning. Want to stand in as goalie for a few?"

"No thanks," Ryder said with a chuckle. "Not against your shot." After only a few years, Noah had already earned his place as having one of the league's hardest shots. "I'm sure Beck or Eli will be along soon."

"Yeah, Eli's on his way. He'll be game." Noah brushed his hair back from his face, and Ryder noticed it was already damp with sweat. He'd apparently been practicing a while already. "As for my shot, it sure wasn't all that lethal last night." He shook his head. "I made it way too easy on their goalie."

"We all did," Ryder said. "It's like coach said afterward. We were undisciplined and reckless. But hey, we'll learn from it and get better, right? It's a long season ahead. Stanley Cups aren't won or lost in September."

Noah's eyes narrowed. "Okay, who are you and what did you do with Ryder?"

He let out a dry laugh. "I probably deserve that. And you deserve an apology. I was an asshole after the game last night."

"Apology accepted. I know losses are tough to take."

"They are, yeah. I want to be a champion, and I put a lot of pressure on myself," Ryder said. "Maybe too much."

"Believe it or not, I do, too." Noah said. "I want to win as bad as anyone. So bad it hurts sometimes. Not that I have to explain myself, but that's why I goof off and joke around off the ice. It takes the pressure off. It gives me an outlet. Like Alex and Seth have their families. And now Trev, too. Colton's working on starting his. Beck's got his budding relationship. Casey has his parties and his girls. Me, I have my video games and comic book conventions." He shrugged. "As much as we all rag on Casey, when he steps on the ice, he gives his all. I like to think I do, too."

"No doubt about it," Ryder said, feeling chastened. "On both counts." He smiled. "One Casey on a team is probably enough, though."

"Probably." Noah laughed. "Me, I avoid the clubs. I'm hoping I'll find a nice geek girl someday."

"I hope you do."

"Yeah. So what's up with you and the news anchor from channel twelve?" Noah asked.

"Nothing much. I kinda blew it," Ryder admitted. "That whole balance thing you were talking about. I'm going to fix it, though."

"Good luck, man," Noah said. "We all like you, even if you do need to learn how to lighten up a little bit."

***

Ryder *wanted* to lighten up, but Jessica still wasn't answering his calls, which added to his overall stress level. How was he supposed to make things right with her if she wouldn't even talk to him? Since he wasn't getting anywhere with the phone calls, Ryder decided to go by the station and try to talk to her after the early newscast. First, though, he stopped by JP's Deli to pick up her favorite sandwich. And one for himself this time, too.

The broadcast had just wrapped up when he arrived, and the pleasant assistant director from his last visit recognized him and said she'd tell Jessica he was there. Sure enough, a few minutes later, Jessica met him in the reception area. She didn't appear happy to see him, though.

"Ryder, hi." She wasn't frowning, exactly, but that sure wasn't a smile, either. "I didn't expect you."

"I've been trying to call for two days," he said. "I'm sure you're angry, and I get that, but I'd like to try to make it up to you. Or at least talk to you and try to explain." Surely, once they talked everything over, she'd understand, right? He wasn't an asshole. He didn't deliberately try to make her feel cheap. He was simply trying to balance different pressures in his life. And apparently doing a lousy job of it. "I brought a peace offering." He held up the bag. "JP's turkey and provolone on Ciabatta with pesto mayo." He gave her a sheepish smile. "And a chocolate brownie."

"You did?" Now she frowned. "That's nice of you, but—"

"Jess, are you ready to go?"

Ryder recognized the interrupting third party as Jessica's co-anchor, a skinny blond guy with glasses. Go where? Surely she didn't have a date with him? Did she?

"Yes, just a minute, Neil," she said. "Did you meet Ryder the other night? Ryder Carrigan, this is Neil Parker, my co-anchor on the news."

"I don't think so, but hello." Neil extended a hand.

Ryder shook it, and found it weak. "Hi."

"Jessica and I were just about to head out to dinner."

So they did have a date. "Oh, well, don't let me stop you, then," he said, trying to save face. "Have a nice time."

At least he'd get to try JP's turkey and provolone sandwich. Hell, he even had two of them. Good thing he was hungry.

***

Ryder, and turkey and provolone from her favorite deli, or Neil and the Chinese buffet around the corner from the station. Jessica had no internal debate as to which of those options she preferred. Even after the events of the weekend, Ryder and JP's won every single time. Yet here she was, with Neil, at Happy China.

"I hope this place is okay," he said. "It's close to the station and we don't have much time, and it's one of my favorite places."

"It's fine," Jessica lied. She didn't care for Chinese food, especially the buffet kind, and she seemed to recall that the restaurant didn't have the greatest reputation. Neil was right, though, in that it was close and they didn't have much time. She'd live with it, even if the smell of the fried oil was already getting to her.

Jessica avoided the chicken dishes, knowing a friend who once got sick on one of them, and instead filled her plate with beef and broccoli and a few vegetarian egg rolls. They looked safe enough. Neil piled his plate high with sweet and sour chicken, apparently unconcerned about the under cooked chicken scare. Hopefully he wouldn't get sick during their late news broadcast.

"Thanks for having dinner with me," Neil said when they were sitting down again. "I've wanted to spend some time getting to know you better. It's been hard since the divorce. Not all women understand the schedule I keep."

"I know how that goes. It can be difficult, for sure," Jessica agreed. Was that the primary reason for his apparent interest in her? He thought she would understand his schedule. If so, it wasn't exactly a ringing endorsement. She bit into an egg roll, and it wasn't horrible. That was her ringing endorsement of the food.

"You've never been married, right?" Neil asked.

"No." Jessica shook her head. "Never found the right guy, and the hours I work are definitely an issue. I do want a family someday, but it may be hard to juggle schedules, although I know other news anchors that manage," she said. "I suppose if my husband worked days, I could be home with the kids, then he'd watch them in the evening while I worked. In theory, anyway."

An arrangement like that wouldn't work with Neil, not that Jessica was terribly upset about that. It also likely could never work with Ryder, given his schedule and the fact that his games were almost all at night. No, it couldn't work with him, and that fact disappointed her. Had he come to the same conclusion, and was it the reason for his behavior the other day? No. More than likely, it was Ryder's intense focus on his career that was to blame. Either way, a relationship between them would never succeed, no matter how attractive he was.

"There's always a way to make something work, if you try hard enough," Neil said. "Unfortunately for me, Marcy wasn't willing to try anymore."

"I'm sorry." Jessica hoped she sounded sincere, and it wasn't that she didn't care. She simply wasn't interested. "So, what kind of music do you like?" she asked, attempting conversation. "Do you like jazz? I went to the jazz festival a couple weeks ago."

"No, I don't like jazz," Neil said. "Country's my thing."

"Oh." Jessica hated country. "What about TV? Do you like medical dramas? Or crime?"

He shook his head. "I prefer comedies."

Great. So far they had nothing in common. "How about books? Do you like to read?"

"Only the funnies in the newspaper, or Consumer Reports when I'm in the bathroom."

Great. There was a lovely image. Jessica surreptitiously reached for her phone and sent an emergency text to Missy. They'd planned for this contingency, and even though Jessica felt slightly guilty for employing the tactic, it was a better option than enduring more of this date, and leading Neil on in the process.

Her phone beeped a minute later, and Jessica looked at it. "It's Missy," she said. "Apparently there's a breaking development. We have to get back to the station."

"Hmm." Neil frowned. "I wonder why she didn't message me." Jessica froze for a second, afraid he might question the ruse. "I guess we better go, then."

Whew. Dodged one there. Thanks, Missy.

CHAPTER THIRTEEN

While Jessica was busy with the late newscast, Ryder was apparently busy making phone calls. She had two messages on her cell phone by the time the news was over, and Missy delivered two more once the broadcast wrapped, calls he had apparently made to the station.

"He's persistent, at least," Jessica said. She wasn't quite sure how to take it.

"Are you sure he's not a stalker?"

Jessica laughed. "Yeah, I think I can safely rule that out." Ryder couldn't possibly find time to stalk women. After all, it would get in the way of winning a Stanley Cup. No, he wasn't a deranged stalker. Just a guy with a messed up sense of priority.

"Well, if he's not stalking you, he's at least very interested," Missy said. "He asked you to call him tonight, no matter what time it is."

Jessica nodded. "I'll think about it." How could she not?

"I hope so. He's always very nice when he calls or stops by here." Missy hesitated. "And Jessica?"

"What?"

"Neil is not right for you. Not at all. And I knew that long before you needed me to execute The Great Date Rescue."

Jessica managed a laugh. "I owe you one for that, definitely," she said. "Believe me, I know Neil isn't the man for me. The problem is, I'm not sure Ryder is, either."

The debate was still unsettled as she drove to Char's house after work.

She was greeted with a curious smile and a glass of wine. "I want details," Char said. "Don't hold back."

"Fine." Jessica accepted the glass and took a sip of wine and helped herself to a seat on Char's couch. It was becoming way too familiar. "Should we start calling this the therapy couch?"

"Call it what you want, but I'm in no position to offer therapy. Have you seen my social life lately?" Char asked with a sardonic smile. "Anyway, tell me about the date. I'm guessing, by your presence, that we can safely assume it wasn't the great dream date."

Jessica choked back a laugh as she swallowed her wine, almost sending it out her nose. "Neil took me to Happy China," she said, once she'd recovered. "Because, you know, nothing says romance better than the $6.99 all-you-can-eat buffet. At least they're open again after that health scare a couple months ago, or who knows where we might've gone."

"Happy China? Seriously?" Char laughed. "Oh, Jess..."

"I know, right?" She let out a laugh. "I seriously

wanted to throw up. But I didn't, so I guess I didn't contract food poisoning."

"Well, that's something at least. But if you have to employ the great date save, that's never a good sign."

Jessica sighed. "No, it's not," she admitted. "I think we can safely rule out Neil as my dream man. We have *nothing* in common. And I do mean nothing."

Char nodded. "Right, and Ryder..."

Boy, she wasn't subtle. "Is someone I have a lot in common with and enjoy spending time with," Jessica admitted. "But does that make up for him making me feel like a cheap slut the other night?" She didn't think so.

"That, no," Char said. "Alone, it's not enough. But other things might tip the scale, depending on circumstances. I mean, he's certainly persistent. How many times did he try to call tonight?"

Jessica didn't even have to stop and think about it. "Five."

"So what does that tell you?" Char urged

"That he's determined. We already established that. He apparently wants to see me, talk to me," Jessica admitted. "I get all of that. But weren't you the one who wanted to castrate him a couple days ago?"

"Castrate, no." Char shuddered. "That's harsh for anyone. I did think he was being an ass, but that's a different story."

"And now you think he's not?"

"Who said that? His actions were completely assholish," Char said. "I've just moved on from that. I think you should at least give him a chance to explain, and try to make it up to you. Don't you think he deserves that much?"

Jessica took a swallow of wine as she contemplated it. Yes, Ryder had been a jerk, but he had apologized right away, and he definitely seemed to want to make it up to her. And up until the fight other night, she very much enjoyed spending time with him. If she slammed the door closed on any chance of a relationship with him, without giving it another try, Jessica knew she'd always wonder 'what if.'

She set her glass down and reached for her phone. "You're right. I'll call him."

"Now? It's almost midnight, Jess."

"Yes, and he said to call him, no matter how late it was," she reminded Char. "I guess I'll find out if he meant it." Maybe it was a little bit of a test, but Jessica would know pretty quickly how serious Ryder was.

**

Ryder watched the ten o'clock newscast preoccupied with what might be going on between Jessica and her co-anchor. When they shared a little laugh over a lighthearted story, he had to begrudgingly admit they shared a good chemistry on-screen chemistry. Ryder hoped it was only that, an on-air thing, and Jessica wasn't serious about Neil Parker. Perhaps their dinner had been a working one only? A guy could hope.

He waited up for half an hour after the broadcast ended, hoping Jessica would return his call. When she didn't, Ryder finally decided to go to bed, but sleep didn't come. How stupidly ironic that he'd jeopardized such a promising thing with Jessica just so he could be well rested before a damn road trip. He hadn't gotten a decent night's sleep since. Yeah, he was an idiot, plain and simple.

When sleep didn't come, he got up and went to his home gym to try to get some time in on the exercise bike. He'd gone about a mile, on an uphill course, when his phone finally rang. Jessica. Maybe he hadn't ruined everything after all.

"Hey." Ryder slowed his pace on the bike. "I was hoping you'd call."

A chuckle came over the line. "Yeah, I think I picked up on that with the five messages you left."

"I wanted to make sure you got them." Hopefully he hadn't seemed too obnoxious. At least she called.

"What are you doing?" Jessica asked. "You sound out of breath."

"Riding my exercise bike. I couldn't sleep." Ryder stopped the bike and got off. "What about you?"

"I am at Char's house, having a glass of wine," Jessica said. "My crazy schedule makes me kind of a night owl."

"I'm sure. At least yours is consistent, and you're not in different time zones a few days out of the week."

"True. I'm sure that's not easy for you guys."

"No, especially going to the west coast." Ryder walked over to the mini-fridge and pulled out a bottle of water. "But just because I worry about my sleep schedule doesn't give me an excuse to be an asshole." There. He'd admitted it.

"You're a very dedicated player," Jessica said. "I knew that before I met you."

"Yeah, but I don't want to be so dedicated that I can never relax or have fun." The rest of the guys did it. Ryder could, too. "Can I see you?" he asked. "Can we talk? Or is it too late for that?"

Jessica didn't immediately answer, causing a hollow feeling to form in the pit of Ryder's stomach. "Not too late," she said. "If it were, I wouldn't be calling. What do you have in mind?"

"Maybe lunch," Ryder suggested. "You don't go into work until about two, right?"

"Around then, yes. I have some flexibility."

"I've got practice in the morning, then some downtime before the game. Can I meet you somewhere? Maybe JP's?" he suggested.

"Didn't you just have that for dinner?" Jessica teased. "I'm going to make a crazy suggestion, but hear me out."

"I'm listening."

"There's a food truck that's always parked at 4th and Alamo, and they sell amazing tacos and gorditas. Meet me there. We can grab some food walk and talk, or find a picnic table," Jessica said. "No crowds."

"I like the no crowds part, for sure," Ryder said. "But what the heck is a gordita?"

"You've never had a gordita?" Jessica sounded shocked.

"I'm from Canada, remember?" Ryder reminded her. "C'mon, what is it?"

"Meet me there at 11:30 tomorrow, and you'll find out."

"Oh, the suspense." Ryder chuckled. "Fine. I'll see you then. Thanks for calling, Jess."

"You, too, Ryder. All five times."

CHAPTER FOURTEEN

For a guy who was normally all hockey, all the time, it was rare for Ryder to count the minutes until practice was over. Especially on game day, following an ugly loss. Under normal circumstances, he'd be one of the last guys to leave the rink, wanting to put in a little extra work. Today, though, he was one of the first ones off the ice and back to the locker room.

"Changing your routine up a little bit today?" Noah asked.

"What do you mean?"

Noah shrugged. "Usually, you'd still be out there, shooting pucks at an empty net, or running skating drills."

"A lot of good that did me in Arizona," Ryder muttered. His shot had been so far off, it hadn't even come close to hitting the net. He had hit a few posts, though. "I guess I am trying something different. I've been wound too tight lately, and I need to loosen up." Fixing things with Jess would go a long way toward doing that.

"Good idea," Noah said. "I'm going to go play some mini golf this afternoon, if you care to join me."

It was Noah's usual pre-game routine. Some of the guys went home for a nap. Others played video games or jammed out to music. Noah played mini golf. Ryder used to think it was silly, but it worked for Noah. "I might do that sometime," he said. "Today, though, I have other plans."

"Oh yeah?" Noah raised an eyebrow. "Do they involve a certain news anchor with long blond hair?"

"They do, indeed," Ryder said. "I'm hoping to fix what I screwed up."

"In that case, good luck," Noah said.

Ryder thanked him and headed to the shower. Half an hour later, he found himself navigating downtown traffic in search of a parking spot. He finally found one, and then found Jessica waiting at the corner she'd told him. Sure enough, there was the food truck, and already a line had formed.

"Popular place, huh?" he asked as they got in line.

"With good reason," Jessica said. "The food's amazing."

"If you say so. I'll let you do the ordering, but you should know that I'm starving. And we have a game tonight. I eat a lot on game days."

"Then we came to the right place," Jessica said. "Are you playing tonight?"

Ryder nodded. "Yeah. I wouldn't blame coach for sitting me after that mess in Arizona, but the regular season starts in less than a week, and we need to get in synch, and get our line combos sorted out," Ryder said. "Am I boring you with hockey talk?"

Jessica shook her head. "No. I know it's your life."

Was that a reference to the previous weekend? He wouldn't blame her. "It's important, for sure. It's my career, and I love the game," Ryder said. "But it's not the only thing in my life, or even always the most important thing."

"Hmm." She didn't sound convinced, and Ryder knew he had work to do, but now it was their turn to order. Jessica ordered both tacos and gorditas, whatever the heck they were, then turned to Ryder. "What do you want to drink?"

"Just water, thanks." He pulled out his wallet to pay, and she waved him off.

"My treat. You might decide you hate it."

"I doubt it." Even if the food wasn't to his liking, the company certainly was.

They got their order, and Jessica pointed to a bench by a tree. "Want to sit over there?"

"Sure." She wasn't the high maintenance sort, that's for sure, and he appreciated that she liked to keep things casual. He still wanted to take her on a real date, though, a fancy one. Assuming he got the chance.

They sat down, and Jessica handed him a gordita, which he learned was beef and cheese and green chilies stuffed inside a baked dough made of cornmeal, called masa. It struck Ryder as a strange conconction, but then again, what did he know about food? Some people probably found poutine and butter tarts to be strange, too. It only took one bite to understand the appeal. "Yum. I could get used to this."

"It's my favorite guilty pleasure," Jessica said. "Even above wine and dark chocolate."

"Really?" Ryder chuckled. "That's high praise."

"No kidding. I try to be careful, though. Gordita

means 'chubby' in Spanish, and if I ate like this every day, I definitely would be."

"Oh, I doubt that," Ryder said. No, from where he was sitting, she was one of the most beautiful women he'd ever seen.

***

Ryder wasn't shy about checking her out, and Jessica didn't mind. He was interested, for sure, proving that what happened a few days ago was not the result of losing interest once the chase was over and the sex was out of the way. That was good to know, since she'd beat herself up about it plenty of times, wondering if she should have played hard to get, or at least exercised a little restraint, and not been so quick to jump into bed with him. Not that they ever made it to the bed, and that was the problem.

"You said you wanted to talk."

He nodded. "I do, yeah. I don't like the way we left things the other day."

"Really, you didn't?" Jessica managed a dry laugh. "Join the club. I can't say I particularly enjoyed being handed a pair of sweat pants for my drive of shame."

"Is that what you call it? Drive of shame?"

"Yeah. It's like the walk of shame the next morning, but worse. I mean, hell, I didn't even rank high enough to make it to morning." The words came out harsher than she intended. Yep. She was still bitter. No doubt about.

"Ouch, you don't mince words."

"Would you rather I lie and pretend you didn't hurt me?" Jessica countered.

"No, of course not. Jeez, I seem to keep messing things up." Ryder let out a sigh. "I hope you don't think it's because I didn't *want* you to spend the night."

Was he serious? "Oh, that thought definitely crossed my mind. Nothing like being shown the door, right after being stark naked and spread eagle for you on the edge of the pool."

"I wanted you so badly, Jess."

"Yeah, I could tell. I still have the scrapes on my legs to prove it."

"Did I hurt you?" He closed his eyes. "If I hurt you, I'll never forgive myself."

She believed him, but he needed to know the truth. "Yeah, you hurt me, all right. Not then, not on the side of the pool. I wanted that like I've never wanted anything. I *needed* it. The scrapes will heal. That's not the problem. I'm just not sure I'll get over what happened after. That's what hurt, Ryder. I felt like you tossed me out the damn curb."

"Christ, don't sugar coat it." He raked a hand through his hair. "That's not what I did. Or at least not what I intended to do. I just..." Ryder's voice trailed off as she shook his head. "You must think I'm a giant asshole. Maybe I am."

"I don't think you're an asshole, Ryder," Jessica said softly. "If I did, I never would have called you last night, and I wouldn't be here today. I think you're a good guy, and you mean well, but you're way too focused on your career to have a relationship right now." She stared ahead at the line of people waiting to get food. "I understand, because I've been that way for seven years. And now... now I'm figuring out something's missing. I want more. I want a relationship. I want a family. I don't want to only be the news anchor for channel twelve. I want it all, or at least more than what I have now." Maybe it wasn't possible to have it all, but there was certainly more to life than emceeing charity auctions reporting on crimes and traffic accidents and the other things that led off the nightly newscast. "And I just don't think you can give it to me right now."

"So you're not even going to let me try?"

He sounded a little like a petulant child, but Jessica was inclined to forgive that. At least he appeared willing to fight for her this time. "I didn't say that. I want to try. I do. But when?" she challenged. "When is your schedule ever going to mesh with mine?"

"We'll figure it out. We'll find a way." Ryder's voice was determined. "Okay, I have a game tonight, and I know you're working. But we could meet after."

"We could," Jessica admitted. "It'll be late, though, and what does that actually solve? We still have an issue."

"You drive a hard bargain," Ryder said. "I'm not giving up, though. We play Saturday, too. Last preseason game, and I probably won't even play in it, but you can come."

"I don't just want to go to hockey games, Ryder." Maybe she sounded bitchy for saying it, but it was time to put it out there.

"I know that. That's not what I'm suggesting. It's just a start." His words came out fast, his voice animated, like he was trying to figure things out on the fly. If nothing else, Jessica gave him credit for trying. "Sunday. No game, and you're off, right?"

"Yes," she admitted. "But aren't you leaving on

Monday?" She'd looked up the schedule, and that's why she knew this wouldn't work. No, it would be another replay of last weekend. No thanks.

"Yes, for Minnesota. The season opener is Tuesday," Ryder said. "I can still take you out, show you a good time... make you see that we can make this work."

"I want to believe that." Jessica wanted it more than she wanted to admit to herself.

"Then give me a chance. One chance. If I screw it up, if I can't convince you, then you can walk away. But at least give me a chance."

He looked so earnest, so sincere, that it was impossible to say no. "Okay, Ryder. Sunday it is. Show me what you got," she said. "And make it good."

His face broke out in a sexy grin. "I'm always up for a challenge. Thanks, Jess. You won't be disappointed."

CHAPTER FIFTEEN

The week passed slowly, with Jessica looking forward to Sunday. She did attend Saturday's game, but Ryder didn't play, so she had little to cheer for, even with a Generals victory. She understood enough about the NHL worked to know that most of the guys who played in final exhibition game would start the season in El Paso. Meanwhile, Colton, Ryder, Trevor, Nik, Casey and the rest of the regulars were given the night off. Their true test would come soon enough, with the start of the regular season in Minnesota.

Jessica was plenty cynical about having any sort of future with Ryder, but was nonetheless determined to enjoy herself on their date. Besides, after her the regrettable date with Neil, pretty much anything would be an improvement. Well, assuming Ryder didn't take her to Happy China for the $6.99 buffet.

When he arrived to pick her up wearing a suit, with an open collar shirt, she figured she was safe, and was glad she'd dressed up as well. "Where are we going?" she asked as they drove.

"Cama Gaucha," Ryder said. "Do you know it?"

Jessica knew it was a popular Brazilian-style steakhouse. "I've never been, but heard it's excellent." It definitely beat Happy China.

"It is. I went once with the guys for a team dinner, and liked it a lot, but decided it would be better on a date with a beautiful woman."

Jessica chuckled as she cocked her head to the side. "What? You mean Casey and Trev aren't your idea of a dream date?"

Ryder laughed. "Believe it or not, no." He looked her right in the eyes. "You are, Jessica. You're who I want to be with."

She wanted to believe it, and so far, so good. He opened doors for her when they arrived at the restaurant, and then pulled her chair out for her to be seated first. Then again, Ryder was a gentleman on their first date, too. Things only fell apart once they had sex. So was that the answer tonight, end things after dinner with a chaste kiss? Maybe, but it wouldn't tell Jessica anything about whether they could have a relationship, and enjoy everything that came along with relationships. No, if they were going to have a chance, Jessica needed to know if they could make all aspects of a relationship work. Not just the sex, which they'd already proven to compatible at, but what happened afterward.

First things first, though. Jessica's immediate priority was figuring out the protocol at a Brazilian steakhouse, where gauchos carried cuts of meat to the table on skewers. They'd been given cards let their server know when they wanted more. "Green side, we want more meat," Ryder explained. "Red side, we're done."

"Sounds simple enough." They ordered wine and side dishes, and suddenly the first cut of meat arrived at their table.

"Picanha," the gaucho said. "Our specialty. Prime cut of sirloin."

It was good, very good, and so was every cut of meat that followed, from the Filet Mignon to the Cordeiro, which Jessica learned was a rack of lamb. "I think you're going to roll me out of here," she joked. She noticed Ryder had placed the red card at the edge of the table, which meant he must be full, too.

"I was about to say the same. I think I ate enough for three people. I guess that probably means we don't need dessert, then, huh?"

"No, definitely not," Jessica said with a shake of her head. "We can go whenever you're ready." *And you can take me home, which will truly decide whether this relationship has any chance at all of lasting beyond tonight.* Right away, she regretted her cynicism. *Jeez, Jess*, she told her herself. *At least give him a chance.*

She owed him that much, and in spite of her own doubts, Jessica wanted it to work. So much so that they arrived back at her house and Ryder walked her to the door, she didn't hesitate to invite him inside.

"I'd love to," he said. "I don't want this to end yet, and I'd like to see your house."

"It's nothing compared to yours," Jessica said of her modest split-level. "But I like it." She showed him around, reminded that she never got as far as the tour at Ryder's house, and they ended up in the doorway of her bedroom.

"Is this by design?" Ryder asked, his eyes twinkling as a smile tugged at his lips.

Jessica couldn't deny it. "You're welcome here tonight, if you want to stay."

"I would like to stay, and I look forward to showing you exactly how much," Ryder said, as his lips met hers.

Any doubt whether she'd made the right decision was erased once he kissed her, and Jessica responded with a hungry need. Yes, she'd allow him to satisfy her in bed, and hopefully he wouldn't disappoint her after the fact.

***

Ryder slipped out of Jessica's bed early, not to leave, but to see what she had in her kitchen. It turned out to be not very much, leading him to believe she wasn't big on cooking, or she hadn't had time to make it to the grocery store yet. He could live with either. He just wanted her in his life, and looked forward to discovering more about her

He managed to find a few eggs and some bread, so he made scrambled eggs and toast, and carried it on plates back to her bed, where she still slept. "Wake up, sleepy," he said.

She did, rubbing her eyes as she raised her head. "Ryder?"

"Yes. Were you expecting someone else?" He looked around. "Whoever it is, I bet I can take him."

"I'm sure you could." Jessica laughed. "I'm not expecting anyone else. I wasn't expecting anyone at all," she said. "I thought you'd be gone. Don't you guys leave for Minnesota today?"

Ryder nodded. "Yes, but not 'til later. I don't

have to leave yet. I want to spend a little more time with you." He held out one of the plates. "I made breakfast."

"Seriously? You're bringing me breakfast in bed?" She accepted a plate from him.

"Well, it's nothing fancy, but I tried." He settled into bed beside her.

"Yeah, I need to go to the grocery store later," Jessica said. "You did okay, though." She took a bite of egg and nodded her approval. I think you make better eggs than I do. Granted, I'm not much of a cook, as I'm sure you'll find out."

She said it as if they had a future, which made Ryder smile. "I look forward to finding out, and to many more breakfasts in your bed, or mine." They ate in silence for a few minutes before the alarm on Ryder's phone sounded.

"I suppose that means it is time for you to leave now." Jessica sounded disappointed.

"Soon," he admitted. "I have a little bit of time."

"Oh yeah?" Jessica raised an eyebrow. "How much?"

Ryder smiled. "Half an hour, give or take." He'd deliberately set the alarm that way.

"Really? In that case, things are looking up." Jessica set her plate on the nightstand beside the bed. "Are you done eating?"

"For now, yes. I think we should use the rest of the time in a more productive way, if you know what I mean."

He knew exactly what she meant. "I like the way you think." Ryder set his own plate aside before pulling her in his arms. He might have to leave soon, but not before he showed her how special she was to him. Balance. Noah was right. It was all about balance, and Ryder believed he'd finally found it.

EPILOGUE

Three months later

Over the next several months, Ryder passed every test. Not that they were true, deliberate tests; more like opportunities to prove himself. And prove himself, he did. Jessica spent the night at his house, even when he had to leave on a road trip the next day. On other occasions, Ryder stayed with her.

When Jessica had the occasional night off, she went to his games to support him. On nights Jessica had to work, she followed the scores from her desk. If Ryder didn't have a game, and was in town, he became a frequent guest at the station, and often brought her dinner from JP's, or one of the other nearby restaurants. And when he was out of town, he called at least daily to check in.

It was a far cry from when Ryder left for training camp and Jessica didn't hear from him for almost a week. Granted, their relationship was brand new then, as opposed to several months old, but still, Ryder truly seemed to be a changed man. As more time passed, Jessica began to view their relationship as something serious, something that had the potential to endure. Before she could say that for certain, though, she did have one test for Ryder.

It came on a chilly—at least by Texas standards—mid-December day. The Generals had just returned from an East coast road trip in which they'd lost two of three games, and fallen five points back from playoff position. Granted, more than half the season remained, leaving plenty of time to catch up, but for an ultra-competitive player like Ryder, who valued winning more than anything else, it had to hurt. Jessica expected him to be in a foul mood when he got back, and she wouldn't have blamed him if he were.

Instead, he arrived at the news station sporting a smile and greeted her with a kiss. "Hi, beautiful. I missed you."

"Missed you, too. How are you?"

"Better now that I'm home," he said. "It was freaking cold in Philadelphia."

"It's not exactly warm here," Jessica said with a chuckle. "Sorry about the game last night." San Antonio had been defeated, 3-0, only the second time all season in which they'd been shut out.

"It was an ugly one, for sure. We got our asses handed to us," Ryder said. "Tough road trip all around, but we're home for a week now. And we get a chance for revenge on Philly when they come here on Monday."

"You'll get 'em then," Jessica reassured him.

He nodded. "That's the plan. So what'd I miss

here?"

He was taking the loss well. Better than Jessica expected. If Ryder had come home in a bad mood, Jessica might have forgotten her little test. In the grand scheme of life, it wasn't all that important. Certainly not something to base a relationship on. But since Ryder was in a good mood, she decided to go for it. "Not much. Just working. I've got a bit of a favor to ask you, though."

"Sure." Ryder didn't hesitate. "Name it."

"I'm planning a birthday for tomorrow, for my friend Char," she said. "Kind of a surprise."

"That's nice of you," Ryder said. "Where do I fit in?"

"Well, she's turning forty, and she's not too thrilled about it," Jessica explained. "To say the least. Anyway, since she works so hard for the Generals Foundation, and cares so much about the team, I hoped maybe you could get some of the guys to show up for the party."

"That's it? You want me to get some of my teammates to come to a party?" Ryder asked. "I can easily do that."

"And maybe help decorate? Like in black?"

He chuckled. "Sure thing. I'm happy to," Ryder said. "After all, she's responsible for bringing us together. That definitely earns a party in my opinion."

Jessica smiled. "Mine, too."

***

Ryder rounded up the guys after practice. One of the perks of being an alternate captain was that it was never hard to get their attention. They probably expected some sort of speech about coming back strong after a tough road trip, and being sharp to open their home stand the following night. Normally, Ryder might give that speech, but today he had other priorities. The game was important, yes, but it was still a day away. Today, he was all about making his girl happy. Balance. Over the past few months, Ryder worked on trying to find it, and showing Jessica he wasn't always all about hockey, and he could love her, too. Now he had the chance to prove it to her.

"I don't normally ask for help," he said. "But today I am. Not like when Trev needed our help to save his daughter. This is nothing like that. It's about my girl, though. I'm trying to do something to make her happy, though it's actually for her friend. Someone who's done a lot for this organization, and our whole community." Ryder went on to tell them about the birthday party Jessica had planned for Char.

"So you want some of us to come to her party?" Colton asked. "Wish her happy birthday, and all that?"

Ryder nodded. "Yes. Can you make it?"

"Sure. Maya and I will be there."

"So will Dani and I," Trevor said. "We wouldn't miss it, after what Char and the foundation did for us."

"I'm free," Noah said. "I'll drop by for a while."

"Count me in, too," Casey said. "I never turn down a party, and besides, she's hot, especially for her age."

Ryder stifled his groan. Now wasn't the time to get into it with Casey. He just hoped his teammate wouldn't make remarks like to the birthday girl.

"Thanks, man, appreciate it." He wasn't surprised at the

support. They were a true team and always had each other's backs. Ryder had little doubt that the tight locker room rapport would help them down the stretch as they fought their way back into playoff position.

Two hours later, he joined Jessica at the club she'd rented for the night to host her friend's party. He found her surrounded by black balloons and streamers. Ryder laughed as he took in the scene. "I hope your friend has a good sense of humor."

"The best," Jessica affirmed. "She'll have a good laugh over this." She handed Ryder a black balloon. "Blow this up, please."

He did as he was asked, tying the balloon when he was done. "You're pulling out all the stops."

"Char's my best friend, and has been for a dozen years. She's worth it," Jessica said. "Are any of the guys coming?"

Ryder nodded. "Yep. Colton, Trev, and Nik are coming for sure, and bringing their significant others. Noah will be here, but he's still flying solo. Jonathan, too, but he's barely old enough to drink. Oh, and Casey. He wouldn't miss a party, and he thinks Char is hot."

"She is hot," Jessica said. "But Casey?" She frowned. "Should I be worried, given his reputation?"

"Nah." Ryder shook his head. "Casey's not a bad guy. He likes his women, sure, but he always treats them with respect when he's with them. And they're always willing and know exactly what they're getting from him."

"Okay," Jessica said. "I doubt he's Char's type, anyway."

"Probably not. You're very protective of your friend."

"I suppose so, but she's worth it," Jessica said. "More than anything, I want her to find someone, and give love another chance. I want her to be happy."

"Like you are?" Ryder urged.

"Yes, like I am. Like we are. That's what I want for Char. To find somebody that's as good for her as you are to for me." She smiled. "I love you, Ryder Carrigan."

It was the first time the 'l word' had come up in their conversations, but it didn't scare Ryder off. He couldn't handle it. He could balance his passion for an incredible woman and his passion for the game of hockey. "I love you, too, Jessica Rowan," he said, bringing his lips to hers.

Keep reading for a special preview of *Making an Impact*, book six in the Men of the Ice series. Coming fall 2016.

MAKING AN IMPACT

Chapter One

Forty. There was life after forty. Charlene Simmons was proof of that, because she'd officially crossed the milestone at 12:22 p.m. Central Standard Time and was still awake, alive and breathing. She was also single, alone, and at this particular moment, depressed.

Perhaps depressed was too strong a word. Char knew people who struggled with chronic depression, and understood the seriousness of it. And no, she didn't have an official diagnosis of depression. She simply wasn't happy about turning forty and being single, so more appropriately, she should probably just be called a moody old maid, and not depressed.

"Moody old maid. There you go," Char muttered to herself as she eased her brand-spanking-new cherry red Mustang convertible into a parking space at the Electric Eel Nightclub. The car had been an early birthday to herself, and why not? She had the money, and worked hard for it, and since had no husband and would probably never have kids, why not spend it on herself?

Char served as the Executive Director of the San Antonio Generals Hockey Club Charity Foundation, a position she considered to be her dream job. Over the past year and half, since the Generals began their first season of play in the National Hockey League, the Foundation had already raised millions of dollars for various charities throughout the San Antonio area. One of the most successful fundraisers to date had been the Bachelor Auction to raise money for awareness and prevention of teenage suicide.

Char used that occasion to arrange a date for her best friend, news anchor Jessica Rowan, with Generals forward Ryder Carrigan. Despite a few rocky moments, the first date had blossomed into love, with Ryder and Jess now being firmly established as a couple. Char was thrilled for them, because Jess deserved the happiness, but sometimes she still wondered where her happiness was. She sure hadn't found it with Graham, since their marriage had lasted all of three years.

Her moodiness over not finding her happily ever after had grown more pronounced over the past several weeks, leading up to the big Four-Oh. Maybe it was silly, getting so worked up over a birthday. Age was just a number after all. That's what everyone said, anyway, but Char was still having a hard time accepting said number as her age.

She wanted to just go home, fix dinner and sit on the couch drinking wine while she watched a sappy movie. Instead, Jess had insisted Char join her at the Electric Eel for a celebratory drink. Fine. Just one, then she was going home and having her pity party, complete with chocolate popcorn.

The club was dark when Char pulled open the door, and she wondered if she had the right place. Why had Jess insisted on meeting at a club, anyway? If they had to do something to commemorate Char's birthday, why couldn't it just be dinner?

"Surprise!"

Char heard the shouts as the lights turned on,

and she found herself facing Jess, Ryder, and a handful of other people from the hockey team, including a few of the players from the team. And a whole bunch of black balloons and streamers.

"Are you serious?" Char asked. "You decided to throw me a surprise party?" She didn't know whether to be angry, mortified, or flattered, that's how screwed up her emotions had been lately.

"Yes, I did," Jessica said. "And don't even bother yelling at me, because it won't change anything." She held out a crown that declared 'Forty and sexy' and placed it on Char's head. "Just have fun tonight. No one deserves it more than you."

***

Casey Denault had a well-earned reputation as a playboy and a party animal, so why should he turn down a good party? Especially when one of his own teammates requested his presence there. Reputation aside, Casey was all about helping his team.

He only knew Charlene Simmons in passing, having met her at a few of the Foundation's events, but Ryder was one of his best friends, and his linemate. His wingman, in essence, since Casey played center. That made his decision a no brainer. When Ryder asked a few guys on the team to attend a surprise birthday party for his girl's best friend, who happened to work for the team, Casey was first in line to accept.

It was a little weird, being the single guy, since many of his teammates were pairing off now, but here he was, nursing a beer and hanging out in the corner until it was time for the big shout of 'Surprise.' Okay, duty done. How long was he supposed to stay? Would there be any other guests? Like, say, any other women? Preferably hot, single women?

Casey knew he'd get some ribbing from the other guys if they were privy to his thoughts, but fortunately they weren't. Anyway, he'd done his part. He'd shown up. Now he'd finish his drink and make his exit; go somewhere a little more exciting. Translation: Some place with a lot more single women.

He didn't want to be rude, though, especially as much as Char did for the Generals organization. Besides, she was one very attractive woman, even if she was fifteen years his senior. That silly crown that she wore, proclaiming her to be 'forty and sexy' sure didn't lie. Maybe it was true what some said about women getting better with age. Casey wondered if it was also true what they said about women and their sexual peak.

Either way, he decided to stay at the club a little longer. "Hi, Ms. Simmons," Casey said, stepping up beside her. He set his empty beer bottle on the counter.

"Call me Char. The other makes me feel old, which is the last thing I need right now." She chuckled once, not a full laugh, and it struck Casey as forced. Yeah, this birthday was hard for her.

"Okay, Char." He flashed his most dazzling smile. Well, most women found it dazzling, anyway. "I'm Casey."

"Yes, I think everyone knows who you are." Another laugh, longer this time.

"Ah, my reputation precedes me. You shouldn't believe everything you hear, though." Casey extended his hand. "Would you like to dance with me, birthday girl?"

**

Char hesitated. She knew Casey's reputation, and it wasn't a good one. Then again, maybe he had a point that she shouldn't believe everything she heard. Whenever the Foundation asked any of the players to volunteer their time for charitable causes throughout the community, Casey was among the first to step up.

She sure couldn't deny he was attractive, with brown hair that hung over his forehead, clear blue eyes, and a boyishly sexy grin. If Casey played on the Generals' top line, rather than being stuck on the depth chart behind team captain and face of the franchise, Colton Tremblay, he'd probably be considered one of the most eligible bachelors in the NHL. Instead, he flew somewhat under the radar, as a second-liner on an expansion team.

"Come on, what do you say?" Casey grinned as he held out his hand. "I don't bite."

What the heck. She had promised Jess that she'd try to have a good time. Char drained her glass wine and reached for Casey's hand. "When you put it like that, how can I refuse?"

She let him lead her to the dance floor. The DJ was playing *1999*, a song Char liked, so it was easy to settle into a dancing rhythm. Casey's moves weren't fantastic, but they weren't bad, either. "Thanks for the dance," she said when the song ended.

"One more?" Casey asked.

Char planned to decline until Bryan Adams' *(Everything I do) I do it for You* began to play. Jess must have had a hand in this playlist. "You sure you don't bite?"

"Only if you ask me to." There was that sexy grin again.

"In that case..." Char settled into his arms for the slow song, which brought back plenty of memories for her. "This was the most popular song my freshman year of high school," she said.

"Which was?"

"1991."

Casey chuckled. "That's the year I was born."

Ouch. "Great. Way to make a woman feel even more like an old maid on her birthday." Char planned to have a chat with Jessica about the song selection.

"Sorry," Casey said. "I didn't mean to make you feel bad, or old, or whatever. You're a very attractive woman."

"You mean for an old maid."

"No." Casey shook his head. "I mean you're very attractive, period. That crown you're wearing doesn't lie."

The crown? It took Char a second to realize he meant the silly tiara on her head. Forty and sexy. "You're kidding, right?" she asked, chuckling.

"Dead serious," Casey replied. "Do I have to kiss you to prove it?"

Books by Michele Shriver

Women's Fiction:

After Ten
Tears and Laughter
Aggravated Circumstances

Contemporary Romance:

Finding Forever
Leap of Faith
The Art of Love
Starting Over
Love & Light
Dissonance
Healing Hearts (coming winter 2016)

The Men of the Ice Novellas:

Playing for Keeps
Crossing the Line
Winning it All
Scoring at Love
Chasing the Prize
Making an Impact (2016)
Breaking the Ice (2016)
Going all In (2017)

Boxed Sets:

Heroes to Swoon For
Spring into Love

Score One For Love
Christmas Pets and Kisses
Spring into Romance
Love Notes
First Glance

Thank you for reading. I hope you enjoyed the story and will consider posting an honest review of this book on the site you purchased it from.

If you purchased this book prior to October 31, 2016, please visit: http://bit.ly/1U1T4iD
to enter to win an autographed San Antonio Generals jersey.

Receive a free digital download of the San Antonio Generals program by subscribing to Michele Shriver's newsletter: http://eepurl.com/323sj

Author's Note and Acknowledgements

I've never played professional sports, so I don't know first hand that singular drive that professional athletes have to achieve their sports' biggest prize. I have, however, seen the Stanley Cup, in all of its glory- and it is pretty glorious. For a hockey player, having their name engraved on the cup is what they play for. Is there room alongside that singular dedication to sports perfection for anything else?

That question became the impetus for this installment of the Men of the Ice series.

I hope you enjoyed reading Ryder and Jess's story and will come back for more books in the Men of the Ice series, featuring Casey and Char (Making an Impact), Noah and Riley (Breaking the Ice) and Trenton and Lauren (Going all In).

This series is special to me, but then again, all of my books are. It's a small world in real life, as well as in books, and the introduction of new Generals prospect Ryan Howton-Canfield now links this series to my novels set in New Hampshire. That wasn't random, though. You can definitely count on seeing Ryan again.

As always, I am grateful to everyone who has helped me along the way in my publishing journey. Your support and encouragement means the world.

This series would definitely not be where it is today without the help of my personal assistant, Valentina Rodriguez. I look forward to more of your ideas.

Michele Shriver writes women's fiction and contemporary romance. Her books feature flawed-but-likeable characters in real-life settings. She's not afraid to break the rules, but never stops believing in happily ever after. Michele counts among her favorite things a good glass of wine, a hockey game, and a sweet and sexy book boyfriend, not necessarily in that order.

Contact:

Website: www.micheleshriver.com
Twitter: www.twitter.com/micheleshriver
Facebook: https://www.facebook.com/AuthorMicheleShriver
Email: micheleshriver@gmail.com

For contests, special gifts, advance reader copies of my books and the chance to hang out and chat and keep up to date on all my publishing news, please consider joining my Facebook group:
https://www.facebook.com/groups/721292531291721/

For more about the Generals and the Men of the Series, visit the website and Facebook page:

Website: https://menoftheice.wordpress.com/
Facebook: https://www.facebook.com/MenoftheIce

CPSIA information can be obtained
at www.ICGtesting.com
Printed in the USA
LVOW12s0019260517
535899LV00003B/216/P

9 781534 664838